Farm Wives
and
Other Iowa Stories

Edited by Marianne Abel

Mid-Prairie Books
Parkersburg, Iowa
1995

Printed in the United States of America.

Book composition by Ireland Design & Publishing,
Cedar Falls, Iowa

Published by:

Mid-Prairie Books
Box H
Parkersburg IA 50665
(319) 346-2048

ISBN 0-931209-57-9

*This book is dedicated to
the life and literature of
Meridel LeSueur*

Table of Contents

Introduction

Marianne Abel

I find homeless stories unsettling. So much of today's short fiction takes place nowhere in particular. I've read dozens of stories that never mention a street, a county or township, no states or countries or geographical features, no local stores, churches, or creeks. Many stories occur only in small, nameless rooms, like stage sets, dissociated from any larger building or socio-cultural framework. Some writers take place for granted today. Or they don't want their work slurred as merely regional. Others think that stories tied to certain locales have a necessarily limited readership. Writing without the context of place inverts literature's classic value to reflect the universal in the particular. What can a universal human feeling be in a generic nowhere?

Some critics say that these disturbing trends mimic larger cultural fragmentations—we don't know where we are in the world. We've lost our place. We have no homes, no families, no communities to go back to. Place is ubiquitous—we all keep moving on. Others blame a publishing industry that prefers national marketing angles. Perhaps these attitudes come from the commercialization of culture itself, spreading from the food industry to the literature we depend on for our contact with the world. Like shifting plate tectonics in the geology of our globe, what we believe literature is capable of no longer includes the stable foundation of place.

Maybe McDonald's stories will be next—the settings will be the same, and only the conversations or storylines will change at each table with different characters. But every McDonald's is unlike every other one. No scene outside the prefabricated window is exactly alike, as long as they keep installing clear glass. Weather changes. Traffic is cars or trucks, or a mixture of vehicles and bicycles and planes overhead, junks or tugs or yachts floating in the canal downwind. Passersby stroll or cruise the sidewalks depending on the neighborhood. Someone could be jimmying a car lock in the parking lot, rightly or wrongly. The concrete block building next to the parking lot might be scrawled with graffiti or an advertisement for a bankrupt grain elevator. Writers should notice these details. They ought to tell us which McDonald's their story happens in.

Place is curious enough. How can we learn to identify what is regional today? I want to turn to literature and art to understand the human side of geography. Travelling in foreign lands without leaving the security of my chair—wherever it is that I sit—I enter the world through books of writing and art. In literature, I test whether I feel at home or at least welcome in someone else's world. As with any country I visit, I count on literature to be didactic and compelling. I ask literature to provide me with characters I can love and hate or at least come to know. I want to bury myself in situations that are believable and yet new, conflicts that seem worth worrying about on any given day. I love language that voices itself off the page. This might be the winning combination of character and place: I meet the people of our world through books before I greet them on their own ground.

I want to put myself in their pictures, in their places. This transference helps me to know my place, to recognize my picture. Stories show me my world for what it is, or could become, or never was. For many of us today, it is fate or accident or serendipity where we land. Is the air worth breathing? Do the flowers smell rank or do they invite us into each others' yards? Is there enough food and clean water? Has the place fostered full lives or just nudged us through a cramped existence? Do songbirds decorate specific trees or are pigeons fenced away from office windowsills? How do we name our rivers, our streets, our public squares? Do the characters in these stories bother to notice their surroundings? Places make people and people make places—good literature and art show us how these two spirals interweave in real life.

When Bob Neymeyer of Mid-Prairie Books invited me to create this collection of stories, I jumped at the chance. I imagined roaming the papered forest floor, like a sprite careening through a deciduous woodland, kicking my way through multicolored leaves, pages and pages of stories that would somehow be about living in Iowa from a woman's perspective. I discouraged him from an anthology of invited stories, mainly because I know so few fiction writers personally. From my work on the magazine *Iowa Woman,* I felt that a random, or at least self-selected sampling would be more intriguing. Last spring, we received seventy stories from all over the country in response to an open call for submissions. The guidelines were simple: previously unpublished, original short fiction set in Iowa—past, present, or future—by women writers anywhere, length at least 6500 words. We read the stories anonymously, without knowing the name or background of the writer.

The task proved more baffling than I'd expected. Like picking corn off the back eighty, I read row after row of well-planted stories, each one a partial representation of some ill-defined whole. I wondered, indeed, what my requirements or standards were. All the writers' names were recognizably female, no problem there. If a male writer disguised his name and got to me through his work, I'd gladly accept it. Writers didn't have to be resident Iowans, or former residents. If someone in New York City or Fairbanks could convince me that their story was an Iowa story, so much the better. Iowa can be the source material for contemporary literature via imagination as well as by residence.

Yet many stories did not mention an Iowa town or place or governor or geographic landmark by name, confirming my worst fears about contemporary literature. Here we explicity called for stories set in Iowa, and Iowa was not clearly in them. On the other hand, this implication that Iowa would be there because the writer was (or used to be) a resident, or because the story had a particular theme, seemed obvious to many other people.

None of the submissions were fantasies or science fiction or mystery thrillers. Do we conclude that Iowa doesn't inspire those genres today? Women are certainly among the leading writers in those forms. Women make up over fifty-two percent of the state's population, and we certainly outnumber men in the regional writing conferences I've attended. Out of the seventy stories, the greatest percentage were veiled memoirs, personal histories of actual lives acted out in particular places that I felt honored to read. The writing wasn't skilled, but the storylines sketched the changing conditions under which we live—and write or create in other forms—as women in the rural Midwest.

One entry came with a confession. The writer had tossed the submission guidelines aside, thinking none of her stories applied. "I didn't have any farm wives meeting lovers on covered bridges, or any country girls dancing in gingham dresses. Not until a few days ago, after looking over the guidelines again, did I realize that I was ridiculously guilty of stereotyping Iowa, and Iowans, although I have lived here my entire life."

She guessed right in an odd way: I didn't pick any of the stories with lovers meeting on bridges or nostalgic memoirs of dancing country girls. I picked the stories that felt like prime corn to me, the way the characters Louella and Jens Hartin, in the story "Forty Acres" by Rose Hamilton-Gottlieb, hand-pick certain ears out of thousands to put away for the next year's seed. The whole crop is critical for seed production, but I harvested the stories that looked right the first time. Since then, I've tried to figure out the other reasons why I like the stories I do.

I work on the Duke Ellington rule-of-thumb. If it sounds good, it is good. No doubt I rejected many a well-crafted story by well-educated and widely-published writers. A good story read on a bad day, or vice versa, is the publishing industry's version of roulette. Another entrant was surprised that I took only seven stories out of seventy. She thought an anthology should be a larger sampling, and she was right, too. There should be dozens of books like this one, for every state and region, including both genders of writers and many genres of literature and visual art.

I chose those stories that appealed to different parts of me at the same time—as a woman, reader, writer, editor, outsider, artist, farmer, lover, sister, mother, daughter, wife, seeker, gardener, anthropologist, historian, traveller. If a story or a work of visual art can reach into my heart and mind on at least half a dozen levels, I know the artist and I are communicating. I also work on the Margaret Mead principle: I can't stand to be bored. If the story holds my interest after three, five, or seven rounds of copyediting and proofreading, I come to believe in abundance again. There is enough to go around; other readers will attend to the work, for their own reasons. This book isn't representative, or scholarly, or exhaustive. It is a collection of stories I like.

What does it mean to be a story or work of art set in Iowa by a woman writer/artist? I asked each writer to describe the crazy quilt of inspiration that holds each story together. There's a family argument mixed with a cultural pattern in the lead story by Hope Burwell, "Farm Wives," about whether women should do field work shirtless. Getting conked on the head by a flying ear of corn and then cursing, "That's it! We're going to California," really happened to Rose Hamilton-Gottlieb's aunt. The photograph "Waiting for Tricks" (on pp. 114) is a candid shot Jo Ann Hendricks Bahr snapped at her mother's kitchen table in Fraser, capturing an entire domestic scene. As each writer/artist explained, writing stories or making visual narratives helps each of them return to places, scenes, issues, and people they've found troubling or provocative.

Not merely realism, these works draw us into an intimate circle where revealment is part of the artistic process, part of history, and part of the narrative line. Lisa Phillips got the idea for the story "Posings" after meeting a photographer at an artists' retreat who explained his project to photograph the city's residents. Both artists are East Coast-born Jews living in rural Iowa. Making other people's private stories public is her job as a journalist and fiction writer, as it is for the photographer. Writing from the Iowa native's point of view, she "wanted to take on the challenge of exploring the questions of art and invasiveness from the other side," she wrote. "What are we outsiders really after? Why can't we ever fit in? Is it the guardedness of rural Iowans or the selfishness of our own attitudes and ambitions, even our artistic sensibilities?" Lisa Phillips' story is a multiple-exposure, beautifully transposing the problems of insider/outsider, observer/participant, and self/other through the characters' differing reactions to one woman's pregnancy.

Etta Worthington admitted that although she placed her story in Iowa, it's not because she has lived here. The daughter of a Baptist minister, her longest friendship is with a woman who was raised in Grundy Center, Iowa. "Her upbringing was very much like mine [in southwestern New York state]—a fundamentalist church being the focal point of life. Like her experience in Iowa, I grew up in communities where farming was quite important. And I went to a very small school, as she did. The terrain of course is different—I had hills—but the people were quite similar," she wrote from where she lives now in Oak Park, Illinois.

"As It Should Be" became a story about the tug-of-war between self-definition and the "shoulds" in the main character's mind. "Even though she is a fairly simple person, she has some important questions that the church and the preacher cannot adequately answer—namely, what is sin, and if God is good, why does he allow retarded children to be born. And if he is all powerful, why doesn't he heal them?" The main character Ardis carries the collective burden of anguish and hope to the tent meeting for relief. Borrowing from the dramas of her own family and childhood, as well as those of friends and church members in two remarkably different states, Etta Worthington crystallized her perception of rural culture into a single human character that speaks.

The published collection proves that one doesn't have to live in Iowa to write something that is believably placed here. Five contributors are native or resident Iowans. Three others call on their rural upbringing in other parts of America—Minnesota, North Carolina, and New York—to sketch fictional settings, conflicts, and personalities that still fit with the locally inspired stories. Regional in the best sense of the term, the stories are obviously not about northern Maine or southern Utah.

Few writers mentioned Iowa directly. I nudged them to add naming words so that we can remember the places where our rivers, our streets, and our towns intersect with our literature. Named or implied, we read through the land itself—its weather and terrors, its sensuous textures and tones, its pleasures and products. Iowa serves as a metaphor: a state of mind, a conceptual place, a collage of longing, history, faith, and commitment.

Although comparable to the rural locale of her native North Carolina, Judith Bell thought Iowa the "perfect" setting for "Vigil" after travelling through here on a road trip. "The unfamiliarity of the place afforded me the remove I needed to write about a personal subject," she wrote about how the setting was important in her story. "In the unvarying openness of the land, I discovered an essential emptiness much like that felt by Iris, the mother. 'Vigil' is a story about the distances, both real and imagined, and the tensile threads that continue to bind us all."

The sense of being alone echoes throughout the book. "Alone" doesn't refer to living without a man in these stories, but to living without a family connection. Even more engaging, living alone is living without a place, without a land to connect to. Perhaps this is something that might be characteristic of first and second generation immigrants (families who settled the Midwest from other parts of America). Retiring to a house in town doesn't offer many rewards for Maude Colgan in "Farm Wives." City life seems grim to Iris in "Vigil."

Louella Hartin's sister describes the pleasant scenery in California in "Forty Acres," but she holds out only the prospect of factory life. Rose Hamilton-Gottlieb based this story on the heartache of an era. "It is about the inevitable conflict within a family who sees its way of life rapidly disappearing. But my subtext is the pull of the land, the sight and sound and the feel and the smell of it," she wrote. "If my own voice is in 'Forty Acres,' it is the sister who writes home from California, who wades in the surf, remembering the feel of fresh-turned earth beneath spring-bare feet, who longs for the sight of a ring-necked pheasant."

The names and places may be connected to Iowa by imagination only, and represent a generic rural Midwest instead. Like the Main Street stereotype founded on a particular street and its culture, the actual Iowa is still recognizable. Iowa is named and pictured here—in places we can find on maps, in grocery stores we can shop in, in supper clubs filled with familiar faces and meals, in farms we've driven by or visited.

The seven illustrations are also visual fictions about Iowa, imprints that spring directly from the artist's daily life. Jo Ann Hendricks Bahr based our cover art "April Fools and Flowers" on her mother-in-law, as well as many other farm wives. "This image characterizes the strong farm women I know, down to the safety pin tacked onto the apron as part of the uniform," she recalled. "I added the belled jester slippers as a way to show that they're not just hard workers; they have a lightness of being that I love, too." Family members, friends, and ideas inform visual art as well as literature. When art is intentionally made from life, the result is more than just an album of family portraits.

One phrase places at least two stories squarely in the Upper Midwest by language alone. "You must be crazy to farm" is a legitimate regional expression with its own delightful brand of logic. It isn't an accidental or off-handed comment, as I mistakenly thought when I first read it. During the copyediting phase of making this book, I asked Hope Burwell to clarify her use of the phrase in "Farm Wives." I heard it as a cynical or snide remark about farming, something like the way I've heard many people deride Iowa and its agricultural habits. She, in turn, pointed out that my motivations sounded more politically correct than editorially precise. We both acknowledged that there is some wry truth to the adage.

In "Farm Wives," the character Maude Colgan says in several

ways that her daughter Ellie must be crazy to farm. As Hope Burwell explained its colloquial meaning, "Maude uses the word the way all my neighbors do when they don't understand something—'but that's crazy.' They might be referring to the fact that we don't let anyone hunt this place, or to the fact that there are people harvesting herbs by hand in our fields. It isn't a comment on sanity as much as on doing/seeing/hearing something out of the ordinary," she wrote.

Burwell works the phrase back on itself later in the story when Maude's friend and neighbor Gert questions whether she should sell the farm and move into town, a common choice of retired farmers. "Don't be a fool, Maude Colgan," Gert says, explaining how staying with Ellie on the farm keeps her busy, physically active, and alive in a way she wouldn't be in town. She hopes Maude will come to her senses and be crazy enough to stay on the farm.

Another clever inversion of the expression occurs in "Forty Acres," when Jens Hartin exclaims, "My God woman, are you crazy?" after Louella suggests they consider selling the farm and moving to California. The implication is that he might be crazy enough to buy the forty acres, but he's not crazy enough to head west. A more distant echo is in "Stray Voltage." Marvella has lost her cat Mata Hari and calls up her neighbor Gert to find out whether the cat's been seen around the neighborhood. "'Mata who?' Gert Phillipson said over the phone in a thin exasperated voice, as if Marvella was foolish. Cats were not of interest to Gert."

These examples (or my explanations of them) aren't linguistically exact, but they point to the telling details that make these stories Midwestern. A. C. Peters, Hope Burwell, and Rose Hamilton-Gottlieb use these phrases naturally—in one case, deliberately—as part of our local language. "Feeding thrashers" is another characteristic regional phrase, referring to the custom of preparing a meal for threshing crews (also in "Forty Acres"). Yet these fictions share elements of rural life in other places, too. In "Posings," as in real life, people must drive forty miles or more away for health care.

Some commonalities between the stories may be characteristics of women's lives and women's writings generally, and not necessarily regional or ruralisms. Nearly all the stories include vignettes of observing, avoiding, and living with the silences of men. Nevertheless, these men are complex and strong characters, capable of gentleness and understanding, yet with personalities and losses of their own. Women talk among themselves, revealing their thoughts more to close friends or to their inner selves than to the men in their lives. In these stories, women think, work, sleep, play, and love passionately—at times, to the point of obsession. Women yearn to preserve and protect what is broadly important, to themselves and the generations around them.

The risks and rewards of communicating with other people crisscross throughout the book. A. C. Peters explains this human backdrop to her story, "Stray Voltage," a fiction that evolved far beyond its origin in a writing exercise using the cat Mata Hari in a story. Personally interested in the lives of rural women, and committed to portraying older women in her writing, A. C. Peters probed how differently men and women seem to approach human relationships. "Marvella is the perfect character to illustrate this sense of frustration and loneliness. She is interested in life, self-aware, she is an artist, she loves her granddaughter and her cat, but she wants to be involved with the larger world outside of the farm. She will not give herself away entirely to anybody, not even Al," she wrote.

"Al has a narrowed sense of perception. He is in many ways Marvella's opposite—stubborn, taciturn, less sociable, forgetful. They each have their own faults, but Marvella is more able to open herself up to the world and embrace it. Al rides off on his tractor instead of risking confrontations, and so he often misses the opportunity to get the things he needs: love, conversation, and companionship. The end of the story is ambiguous because the nature of long-term relationships seems to me to be one of ambiguity and incomplete resolution."

Television as a source of contact with the world is another, perhaps unexpected, common theme playing in the background. In "Farm Wives," Maude Colgan expects her daughter to have heard about feminism on TV and to have applied—or at least thought seriously about—how feminist issues expand the range of possible decisions she could make. Judith Bell portrayed her own experiences in "Vigil." The TV drama "Thirtysomething" served as the communication link with her mother after direct conversation failed.

"I would imagine my mother watching, recognizing the parts of me I would want her to see in these characters' lives. I would note the things that would confuse her, all problems and attitudes that were a very real part of my experience," she wrote. "And that through her watching, I would no longer need to explain my world as it has come to be at a remove from my family of origin and my rural beginnings in Piedmont, North Carolina." Television weather reports have replaced the radio heard in "Forty Acres," but the reliance on outside experts for information, news, and cultural change is still there.

From the writer's craft standpoint, newspaper reports served as essential inspirations in "The Flood Summer" and "Farm Wives." Patricia Stevens reflected on three separate articles to write her story about how grandparents raise their children's children. "These [clippings] caught my attention, I think, because I could not help wondering what it would be like to believe you were finished with childrearing and ready to start the 'good life' and then be faced with raising yet another generation," she wrote. Not just Delia's fortune or the result of a flooded summer, Patricia Stevens explores what have now become American themes—missing and abandoned children, violence, single grandparenthood, and the repercussions of social dislocation.

One of Hope Burwell's impulses in writing "Farm Wives" was also critical. *The Des Moines Register* had reported "that Iowa had more people twenty-eight-years-old or older living at home with parents than any other state." This is an Iowanism, but the way it was editorialized caught Hope's attention and worked its way into her story. "The tone of the article was condescending, implying that adults who lived with parents were either victims of a weak economy, or emotional cripples," she wrote.

"We'd just had a seventy-year-old friend of ours to dinner. I'd spent the last ten years watching him learn to live without the mother who had been his life-long companion before her death. Feeding Bruce and listening to his stories about times when his mother was alive made me think about all of the rural people I know who live with their parents for all but the aging years of their own lives. Taking out the story and reworking it allowed me to think about those relationships, to test and finally to challenge our cultural assumptions that people who never leave their parents' homes are somehow damaged or lacking."

Charming, captivating, funny, and full of ideas, these fine fictions ask us to stand back from the field and contemplate how contemporary art can feed us. Reaching into the blue-and-white speckled roaster on the stove as if into Pandora's box, we find difficult questions mixed in with the carrots and potatoes. Who writes and publishes our literature? Who reads it? How do we tell others about our lives? Who makes our art? *Farm Wives and Other Iowa Stories* presents some not-so-simple answers. Wedded to the land and all the life around us, we come to understand the reasons why we leave and why we're crazy enough to stay.

Thanks to the writers whose work creates this volume, and to Jo Ann Hendricks Bahr for her illustrations. I am indebted to Hope Burwell and Beth Simon for our discussions about being crazy to farm. Thanks to the late Dorothy Albertson, Carol Bly, Jan de Rooden, Johnny Rolf, Jolene Rosauer, Maureen Seamonds, and the women of Iowa Woman Endeavors, Inc., who've helped me learn what it means to be from Iowa. My sincere appreciation goes to Bob Neymeyer of Mid-Prairie Books for inspiring and producing this wonderful book. And dear thanks to my husband Harry Lipschutz for his support and encouragement.

Farm Wives

Hope E. Burwell

For Ellen Pearson

Up along the north fence line the Hereford bull stretched against four strands of barbed wire for a wave of newly mown alfalfa. "Better 'mind Ellie 'bout that fence again," Maude Colgan muttered over the engine of her seventeen-year-old Volkswagen Beetle. A flurry of chickens from beneath the shade of a battered '72 Chevy pickup evoked a minor smile. The sight of her daughter cut the smile short.

Eleanor made her way from the pump house to the barn, a full five-gallon bucket in each hand. She walked, back straight, head high, arm and shoulder muscles bulging. She wore men's Red Wing boots, a pair of faded, often-patched jeans, and from the canvas belt at her waist to the Three Rivers Coop cap on her head, nothing. Stopping as the car blocked her path, she glanced past her mother's face to the three bags of groceries in the back seat. "Awfully hot, isn't it, Mama? Hope you got some ice cream. Leave the car out, I'll bring the groceries in a sec." Before Maude had a chance to speak, Eleanor turned, resuming her evening chores.

Rusty hinges kept Maude inside the steamy little car. She opened her mouth to call Eleanor. A sun-bleached pony tail cascaded through the hole in the feed cap, down a sunbrowned back. Maude clamped her mouth shut. Swiveling in her seat, she faced the door, and palms flat, banged against it with a motion that began in her buttocks. Triumphantly, she picked her purse up from the front seat, reached for the carton of ice cream she had insisted be triple wrapped ("I'm not serving Borden's vanilla porridge, young man. Insulate that box properly."), and walked up the brick path to the house. Seventy-seven years showed in the stutter of her right hip. She put the ice cream in the kitchen freezer, and picked up the conversation she'd been having with her husband since shortly after his death eleven years earlier.

"She's gettin' crazier and crazier, Frank. Never should've let her quit college." She started supper: pounding pepper into beef, peeling vegetables, and thinking, as she had in fits for years, about the day she'd found Frank beneath the Farmall.

It was spring, and he'd been turning the field for the first time, tucking last year's corn stubble in under fine, unglaciated northeast Iowa topsoil. Maude thought for the millionth time: he must've had that pair of little front wheels cranked too tight when he hit the old row mound. Must've hit that hump, and when the front end tipped, there was nothin' to catch him. She saw again the old-fashioned tractor, a big red tripod like a child's tricycle: two small wheels stuck way out front on the engine's nose, two enormous ones framing the seat, and only hope to keep the thing balanced.

Eleanor had come home from college to help with the funeral. Four days later, when she ought to have been getting back, she'd refused to go. "Daddy would want that field planted, Mama," she'd said. "You know how much he hated an unfinished job. I'll get the seed in the ground and then I'll go back." But Maude had heard the proprietary tone in her voice.

"And who'll harvest it?" she asked.

Eleanor tossed her head like a spring filly. "I will, Mama. Who else?"

Maude snorted. "Frank, last thing I wanted was to move into town. But, if I had, would she've gone back to school and finished that teaching certificate? Sometimes I think she was just waitin' for you to go, old man. Took to farming this place like it was all she ever wanted. Now look at her."

The screen door banged. Eleanor plopped two bags of groceries on the oak table. "What's Daddy got to say for himself today, Mama?"

Maude went on slicing one of last year's rubbery carrots. "Says you got down too much hay for one woman to get up 'fore it rains, girl."

Reaching into the blue-speckled roaster for a piece of raw potato, Eleanor snorted. She got a slice, and, the instant her pink nipple entered Maude's line of vision, a smart smack on the knuckles with the dull side of the knife. "Ouch! Mama, what're you so grumpy about?" Then, staring at the roaster, she exclaimed, "Oh Mama! You're not going to put a roast in the oven tonight? Not tonight, Mama! It's too hot."

Maude reached for another carrot. "Don't s'pose that ought to matter to a half-naked woman."

She felt Ellie stare at her back, and then heard the refrigerator door open. Ellie poured a glass of water from the chilling bottle, and left the room. In the darkened living room, shades pulled to the window sills against the heat, she turned on the television. The six o'clock weather report competed with Maude's conversation.

"Francis Kelley Colgan, what am I supposed to do about that? Damn you. Twenty-five years of no babies and then you give me that one when I'm too old to want her. Grew up wild. Now you see what's come of it. Won't hire help. Walks around here naked as the day she was born, 'er almost. S'pect that'll come next."

From the depths of the living room, Eleanor's chuckle intruded. "No it won't, Mama. I don't care much for the thought of sand burrs in my fanny."

Maude banged the lid on the enamel roaster and pushed it into the oven. "Eavesdropper," she mumbled.

"Daddy's wrong, Mama," Eleanor said lightly, switching off the news and heading back across the kitchen to the pantry Frank had turned into a bathroom. "No rain for three days. I'll get the hay up in good time."

Maude headed for the garden, letting the back door slam.

From her squat between rows of tomatoes, she watched Ellie head for the cabless John Deere, the one with the wide-set front tires she had insisted replace the murdering red Farmall. Ellie crawled up, settled easily into the deep green seat. Watching the ground over her right shoulder, she backed the tractor to the rake, got off, dropped the pin hitching the two implements together, and remounted. The gear shift sucked into place and she headed for the hay field. The old rake clacked behind her, tumbling down the drive and tossing gravel into the air. Staring, Maude missed a buttonweed for which she was reaching and came back with a tender young tomato plant.

"For God's sake, Frank, she's goin' out in the field like that. Look at her, will ya? Paintin' walls, pickin' stalls like that, that's one thing." She watched the hay roll bottom side up where tomorrow's morning sun could finish the drying. Like mole excavations, long humps of green riddled the field in the tractor's wake. Eleanor rounded a corner far up on the east hill and her mother groaned, "Oh, sweet Jesus." Perhaps her eyesight wasn't what it once had been, but she could tell that was a woman, a bare-chested woman on that tractor. "Oh Lord, Frank," she swore, "what if she takes to workin' the roadside field like that?"

It felt as if the sun had set right there in the kitchen. They couldn't eat in that heat, Maude conceded. She carried plates and silverware out to the tall picnic table Ellie had built for Mother's Day. When the rake pinged gravel into the LP tanks next to the house, she stirred Nestle's Quik into two glasses of cold milk, added a scoop of ice cream to each, and carried them through the twilight to the table. The roar of the tractor hushed. Eleanor swung one leg over the steering wheel and, leaning against the fender, reached for a hose on the gas barrel six feet off the ground.

"Supper's ready, girl." Maude called.

Eleanor jumped away from the engine's roiling heat waves, and headed across the yard. "Oh, Mama, Brown-cows, how nice." She reached for a glass.

Maude smacked her hand. "You go put a shirt on. I never, not in all the years I lived with him, let your father come to a table bare-chested and I'm not about to let you come that way either."

Eleanor studied her mother's face and gave in. She returned in an over-large white shirt, the excess fabric knotted at her slender navel. Her mother humphed, "Leastways it's clean," and eyed her daughter as she folded her long legs under the picnic table. Just as Ellie opened her mouth to speak, Maude interrupted, "Don't s'pect you ought to say grace after what you been up to these last few days," and passed the platter of roast beef and root vegetables.

Eleanor laughed softly, "I don't suppose She'd mind, Mama. She made me this way, after all."

"Now that's enough." Maude set her fork down with a thud. "I will not have you talkin' that way at this table. Goin' bare naked in front of God and everybody, that's one thing. Won't have you callin' names and pokin' fun, too."

Eleanor chuckled again, "Bare naked is redundant, Mama. Now what's the matter with you? You act as if you've never seen a pair of breasts before."

Maude shoved a bite of carrot into her cheek, out of the way of her tongue. "What's the matter with me? Lord, girl, yeah I seen 'em. I seen yours 'fore there was anything to 'em. And I seen 'em again when they was just little squishy nubbins on your chest.

And I seen 'em when they was a whole handful and I had to wrestle you into a brassiere. I hoped that was the last time I'd see 'em. Point is, what if somebody else sees 'em?"

"Well, what if they do, Mama? I suppose anybody who knows me knows I've got them."

"Frank, will you listen to her! My God, Ellie, are you heat-addled? You can not go paradin' yourself around here like, like somethin' from the *National Geographic*."

Eleanor sighed. "Mama, I am not parading around. I don't intend to go into town shirtless. I don't even plan to answer the door without a shirt on. But it's hot, Mama. For thirty years I've envied men while my shirt clung to me like a wet dishrag. Well, I'm not going to envy them anymore. Not on my own farm, anyway."

It's not your farm, Maude thought in a flash of anger. She stared for a moment at her daughter, and then returned to eating. They went on in silence, finishing first helpings, taking smaller seconds. "What's come over you, Ellie?" Maude asked finally. "Eleven years you been workin' this place and 'fore this summer I never seen you do such a thing."

Eleanor drained the last granules of Quik from her glass and stood. She paused, shrugging her shoulders slowly, for the briefest second uncertain. "I don't know, Mama," she confessed, then sighed. "Sorry to leave you eating alone, but Amelia just went into the barn. Thought when I checked her this noon that calf would be here by now. Gotta go check her again. Thanks for supper, Mama." She turned and strode through the settling darkness.

"Well, Francis, there she goes. Proud as your mother and nearly as off her scooter. Oh, I know, she's a good girl. But crazy. Gettin' crazier."

She turned to survey that part of the farm she could see from the picnic table: a vegetable garden, Ellie's perennial beds, a fourteen-acre alfalfa field and thirty acres of pasture, the oak and hickory treeline marking the Maquoketa River. While she watched, a golden blanket settled down over the field Ellie had made last week. From the timber's edge, the deer herd began to flow smoothly out of the dark. She counted six, seven, eight, brick-red white tails before turning her head slowly toward the barn. Leaning on an open half-door watching the deer, Ellie smiled silently back.

When he died, people said Eleanor Colgan would never make a go of her daddy's place. They said she was too queer to marry and, without a man around, the bank would have the farm in a year or two. It had taken every day of the nine years left on the mortgage, but Maude could still remember the day Ellie stood at the kitchen stove, all dressed up in her going-to-the-bank navy skirt and pumps and starched white blouse, grinning. She'd struck a red and white farmer's match across her bottom, and when it flared, lit the mortgage papers. She stood there until she'd had to drop them on the polished white range. She'd turned to her mother then, offering the deed. "There, Mama. Only banker breathin' down my neck now is that J. D. Billows."

"Thinks she can do anything, hates herself when she can't," Maude whispered into the twilight. "First time the baler broke a sheer pin she come in the house wantin' to know where you kept the machinery manuals. How was I to know, I asked her. Out in one of the shops, I guessed. I looked out the window later and there she sat in the field, that book in her lap, scratching her head and talkin' to herself. Next thing I hear that clunk clunk clunk and there's bales comin' out the chute again. Frank, that girl can make two-hundred-and-fifty bales of hay in a good day and get them all stacked in the mow before dark. But she's got to be a little crazy to do it. Don't nobody farm alone when they got other options. Why won't she hire some help, Francis? What's she provin'?"

She could almost hear Frank's, "What's so crazy, Maudie? If she was a man you wouldn't think farmin' this place was crazy. Wouldn't think goin' shirtless was either . . ." The pride that had run in his voice like syrup when he talked about their only child irritated her. Like he'd had more to do with makin' that young woman than she had.

She rose finally, cleared the table calling, "Here kitty kitty kitty," and scraped roast beef scraps onto the ground. She carried dishes to the house and was running the water when Eleanor came through the back door interrupting Frank's inquiries about the health of the livestock.

"Here, Mama. Let me wash, get some of this grease out from under my fingernails. Amelia's going to do it tonight, but it'll be a while yet." They stood side by side, quietly washing and drying dishes, immersed in their own thoughts until Maude interrupted.

"Amelia's had half-a-dozen calves, Ellie. There's no need for you to spend your evenin' in that birthin' stall."

"I know, Mama. But there's something magical about the way

those great big calves come swooshing out, the way their eyes pop open with the first mama-moo."

They fell silent, Maude considering all the ways Ellie found wonder in the farm, remembering the day she'd come upon her, nose buried in a handful of loamy black compost. At supper that night she'd said it made her feel like God to stir the compost heap, to realize she could make dirt. Maude had thought it a crazy thing to say, but she'd held her tongue. Girl was entitled to her notions.

"Mama?" Ellie penetrated the extended silence so quietly that Maude turned to look at her. "Does it bother you, Mama, that I'm not married?"

Maude was completely taken aback. Married? Ellie married? It hadn't occurred to her. Not once. Not even when she was little, and pink. For the first time she wondered, why hadn't it? "Lord no, girl," she said more gruffly than she'd intended. "Whado I want with a man around this house, missin' the toilet and leavin' his socks scattered in every room?"

Laughing, Eleanor handed her mother a freshly rinsed glass.

The girl had started this conversation weeks ago, and piqued Maude's curiosity. She'd come home from town one afternoon somber, everything pulled in close to her chest. It had taken her three days to come out with it. They'd been putting in the garden, Maude stretching the row string from side to side, and Ellie punching quick holes in the soil with the dibble. Ellie had been quiet too long and finally Maude had grumped at her, "What'd you see in a little town like Strawberry Point to make you so drawn in, girl?"

Eleanor looked up suddenly, focusing on her mother. "Hm," she'd grunted, rolling broccoli seeds in the palm of her large hand. "Doesn't sound like much, I don't suppose, Mama."

"Well," Maude said, jabbing one end of the string stake into a new row, "then shouldn't be so hard to tell."

Ellie nodded, stepping over the string to reach for the packet of green beans Maude handed her. "I don't know, Mama. I just been thinking. Drove past Anna Meck's the other day. The house has a new coat of paint, and somebody was out cutting the hay field. I thought, well finally, Anna's quit playing the widow and is getting back to living. She's only two years older than I am, Mama, she could work that farm if she wanted to. So, I drove down her lane to give her a welcome-back hug. But when I looked again, it wasn't Anna on that tractor. It was Byron Kelly. And I wondered if Anna is still sitting in that house feeling helpless, or if she's getting ready to marry Byron. Makes me mad, Mama. Makes me wonder why Gert doesn't just go in there and give her a good shake. Gert's been living without a husband for fifteen years now. You'd think her daughter would take a lesson."

Maude listened quietly. It was a long speech for Ellie, a sign that something beneath the words troubled her. Maude had known that, like her daddy, it would take Ellie a while to get it out, and she'd been waiting impatiently. Now here was this question, sudden, like water out of the pitcher pump after long patient pulls on the handle. Did it bother her that Ellie wasn't married? Did it bother Ellie? That was the question.

While Eleanor scoured the sink, Maude fingered the black chip in the roaster's lid and watched her daughter, sucking on the unasked question like a lozenge. Her hip sockets began a dull, sour ache and she glanced out the window to the western horizon. "Don't care what the forecast is, girl, it's going to rain 'bout this time tomorrow. You got more than two hundred bales down out there. You better see if you can find some help in the mornin'."

Eleanor sighed. "'Bout three hundred I'd say, Mama. But it's all raked. I can start baling soon as the dew dries. I'll park the last rack in the machine shed if I don't get it in the mow before the rain comes." She turned, stooped, and hugged her mother warmly. "I'd have a lot of wet hay if it weren't for those hips of yours, wouldn't I, Mama? You take some aspirin, or a little brandy, and get to bed. I'm going out and watch Amelia."

Maude watched her go, stood quietly in the middle of the big kitchen deciding what to fix for tomorrow's lunch. Something cool but filling. That girl would be working like three people all day long. She'd pull the three-implement train endlessly around and around the field. Bales would chug out along the bale chute and bunch up on the hayrack behind it. Then she'd get down off the tractor, climb onto the rack, carry the bales back one by one, and stack them in alternating layers. Then down off the rack and back up on the tractor again for another half-a-dozen bales. It wasn't especially hard work, bale by bale, Maude thought, almost nostalgic for her own days driving the baler while Frank worked the rack, forcing him to trade with her every three or four rounds. But by the end of the day, Ellie would have lifted and toted and stacked and unstacked and carried and stacked again twelve-thousand pounds of hay.

From the sleeping porch where she and her husband had shared many humid Iowa nights making love or lying close waiting for a breeze, Maude listened to Ellie moving in the kitchen. She heard the sounds of the drip coffee maker readied for morning, the chilling bottle filled and put back in the refrigerator, the back door shushing tight again. Propped on one elbow, she watched her daughter cross under the fluorescent yard light and enter the golden light of the barn, again. When she woke at one-fifteen, the light in the birthing stall was still on. She woke again at two to the sound of the back door closing.

"Ellie?"

"Yeah, Mama," she sighed. "Twins. Heifers. One of them stillborn."

Maude winced.

In the doorway to the sleeping porch Ellie said softly, "Amelia's all right though. 'Night, Mama."

"'Night, daughter."

The western sky boiled with gray-green clouds, and Ellie paced. Maude watched her from the bathroom window. Over to the tool shed for a fresh can of grease, back again for the grease gun she had apparently forgotten, back to the baler. She tugged at the frozen nozzle on the grease gun, and then frustrated, threw it across the gravel to the machine shed. She stared at the sky again, sniffed the air like a worried deer, and stomped over to retrieve the dented aluminum cylinder. Maude heard her swear as she levered the gun's nozzle on the baler, straightening out the bend she'd caused with her tantrum. She slammed grease into each zerk on the baler while Maude wondered, "What's the matter with that girl, Frank? Isn't just the rain. She's had wet hay before."

But, she thought, watching Ellie nurse the knotters into position, maybe it is just the rain. That girl took more pride in her work than she ought. Maude had caught her, late last January, breaking a sweet green bale of alfalfa to throw to the cows. She was standing in the snow in her insulated coveralls, in front of a feeder crowded with white faces, a slab of alfalfa in each hand, grinning like the winner of a spelling bee. She had turned at the sound of her mother's car door and held the pads of dry, beryl fodder in Maude's direction. "Look at that," she'd said smugly, "middle of winter and the buds are still purple." And they were too, Maude thought.

Eleanor looked up at the sky for the fifteenth time, turned her back, and climbed onto the tractor. "Damn it, Frank," Maude mumbled. "I wish I could still work a hayrack. Whattaya s'pose she'd do if I called Byron Kelly and he just showed up here rarin' to work?" She could almost hear Frank's answer, "Don't you do it, Maudie."

When the clunk clunk of the baler had been silent for too long, Maude set her mending basket on the couch and went to the window. The slatey wash that had been the western horizon was a solid umbrella, a bowl upside down over the farm, closing out light, leaving everything in khaki shadows. For the third time that morning, Ellie lay flat on her back under the bale chamber. "Knotter's being cantankerous, Francis," Maude muttered and moved back to her mending.

Later, the tractor chugged into earshot and Maude looked up to see the day's second precisely stacked mountain of hay move by the window. Through the trees on the other side of the hayrack she glimpsed a lightening sky, flannel gray, the green threat of tornado washed into the east. Nearly an hour later, she shuffled out through the barn and stood in a stall doorway until the last rectangle disappeared up the elevator, thudding onto the boards above her head. Ellie jumped down off the rack, climbed onto the tractor, and disengaged the power-take-off, rending the afternoon with sudden silence. She looked at her mother in the dark doorway.

"You come on in and have some lunch now," Maude called.

Hiking a shoulder, Ellie wiped the sweat and leaf shreds from her face onto her grimy workshirt. "Can't, Mama," she said.

Maude bristled. "Don't 'can't' me, damn it. Get down off that tractor and get in that house. You didn't eat but coffee, and the sky's clearin'. You'll get that third rack in after you got some food in you."

Ellie followed her mother's gaze over her own shoulder to the western sky. Nothing like blue in it, but nothing like immediate rain, either. She sighed, kicking her legs over the steering wheel.

If Maude had hated anything about Francis Colgan it was his silences. For days, it seemed to her, he could go on speechless, brooding, like a bank of ashen clouds looming on the horizon. But she'd counted herself lucky, too. His storms blew over, moved out across the fields eventually, leaving her and Ellie unharmed, but also uninformed. She wasn't going to make the mistake of getting used to living with that again. She let Ellie put away half a dozen slices of raw kohlrabi and a serving of honeyed peas and braised walnuts before interrupting her broody quiet. "What's eatin' at you, daughter?"

Eleanor looked surprised to find her mother at her right elbow. "Nothing, Mama," she said softly and forked up another bite of peas and walnuts.

"You remember how stony your daddy got when he was bothered? Livin' with him then was like livin' in the Old Testament. Too quiet and wrathful."

Ellie looked up again. "Mama," she warned, "I don't think you want to have this conversation."

Maude squinted at her daughter. Now what the hell did that mean? "He wasn't like that when I married him, you know. It grew on him, like grape vines on a cedar tree. After a while he was more silence than man. I'd rather he'd talked—even if he was plottin' murder. Nothin' he thought would have stopped the way I loved him." That worked, she thought smugly, watching the weight of her confidence settling on Ellie's shoulders.

"I've been thinking about sex, Mama."

Maude swallowed hard. Well, Francis, I asked. "Sex?"

"Uh-huh."

"And what're you thinkin' about it?"

Ellie shrugged and nudged her empty lunch plate more deeply into the table so she could rest her folded arms. "I'm thirty-two years old, Mama," she said quietly, "and I'm still a virgin."

Oh Lord, Frank. Did I need to know that? "Uh-huh," Maude answered.

"Is there something wrong with me, Mama?" Ellie asked.

"'Cause you're still a virgin, girl? No. I don't think there's anythin' the matter with that. I was one too, you know, 'til I married your father."

"But, Mama," Ellie said hopelessly, "you married Daddy when you were, what, twenty? I'm nearly twice that, Mama."

"Thirty-two ain't twice twenty, Ellie," Maude said briskly, almost wishing she hadn't pushed herself into this conversation. "But, even if it is, your time's comin'. That J. D.'s been interested a long time."

Ellie puffed her lips together, like she did when she was really frustrated, and blew out a long stream of air. "Mama," she said, "I'm not going to marry J. D. That's just it, I guess. I don't have the slightest interest in getting married, Mama."

"Well," Maude said bravely, "ain't nothin' anymore says you got to be married, Ellie." She thought that might at least bring a quick, surprised smile. It didn't.

"I know, Mama. Nothing except the fact that I'm just not interested."

Maude simply watched her daughter then, a little lost in what she was getting at.

"Mama," she said finally, "why don't I have the least desire to, well, couple? Not even a twinge of it, Mama. Seems like I'm just filled up. When I wake up in the night, longing, well, it's not for another person, Mama. It's for more sunlight in the living room in the winter, or fence rows made completely of round, straight wooden posts, or the nerve to try triticale next spring instead of soybeans again."

A cool, threatening breeze flapped the muslin curtain into Eleanor's plate. She stood quickly, glancing out the window at a repeat of the morning's horizon. "Shit," she said, and left her mother sitting at an empty table.

Maude paced the house from window to window watching Ellie and the storm and thinking about the conversation. Where had all that come from, she wondered. Maybe Anna Meck *was* getting married. All the girls in Ellie's class were, some for the second time. Only other unmarried girl in town was Hattie Kennedy. For a while she'd lived with that woman she'd brought home from college. But that's not it, she thought. Ellie's not worryin' 'bout bein' like Hattie Kennedy.

She stood at the picture window, whip-stitching a patch onto the right thigh of a pair of Ellie's jeans. Ellie used that side to bounce bales on when she stacked. Frank never wore his jeans out like that, never needed any muscles below his waist for makin' hay. He split the seam across his shoulders. "What'd happen, Francis, if I sold this place?" Maude asked. "I could move into one a them senior citizen's apartments. And Ellie, s'pose she'd marry J. D. then?"

"No it DON'T bother me she ain't married." She bit her thread behind the knot. "Bothers her. I can tell."

"Ought 'ta bother her. Come to think of it, isn't normal.

Thirty-two years old, sexless, childless, nothin' but this farm to hold her."

"J. D.'s land ain't as good as this, but the house is newer. Bigger. Ellie'd have plenty to do."

Later, after Maude finished graining the livestock, she stood in the doorway shadow at the base of the bale conveyer, watching. Ellie slammed bales onto the elevator, muffling the sound of recurrent thunder so much that when the rain hit her back and her head in fat greedy drops, it surprised her. Maude watched her turn toward the wind as if to fight, to talk back. Instead, just as the storm roared over, she yanked her shirt off, letting the rain rinse the chaff from her body.

In the middle of July, the freezer aisle at the new Oelwein Fareway made a wonderful place for old women to stop and catch up. Maude leaned her elbows on the grocery cart's red plastic handle. Gert leaned back against the frozen pizza case. "Ellie get her hay up?"

"Most of it," Maude answered. "Raced that demon all day long. Had a couple dozen still on the rack when the sky split."

Gert shook her head in affectionate wonder.

"Byron get Anna's hay in?"

"Most of it. But then he probably had a lot more down than Ellie. Those big machines make 'em think they can do anything. Ellie does it smarter. Chews her food in small bites." Gert looked down, scooted the cuticle of her right index finger with the nail of her left.

"What's troublin' you, Gert girl?" Maude asked. They'd gone to school together all eight years in a row; certain liberties were permitted.

Gert sighed. "Anna." She looked up. "I'm going to have to move in with them girls and take care of 'em, Maudie. Anna, well she can't take care of that farm to save her life. She come over cryin' last week, says the baby's got to have senior graduation pictures and the check bounced. I took that checkbook outta her hand, Maudie, and why, that girl's been just writing down the checks and never subtracting a cent."

Maude didn't know what to say. It seemed impossible to her: 1986 and the girl was that helpless? Didn't she ever see television; hear 'bout those feminists? For Gert's sake, she clucked sympathetically.

"You're a lucky woman, Maude Colgan. You raised that daughter a yours right. Anna ought to be takin' care of me the way Ellie takes care of you," she said. "'Stead I got to leave the house I been in sixty years and go do her books and her hiring for her."

Maude shifted her weight from one hip to the other. "What about when we're gone, Gert?"

Gert pulled a loose hair pin from the silver braid curled in the middle of the back of her head and replaced it more snugly, eyeing Maude all the while. "I'm just hopin' Anna's married again by then, Maudie. If she ain't when I start feelin' my time comin', I'm gonna insist she take what she can get for that farm and get herself into town."

Maude nodded, and stared at the black boxes of Red Baron pizza behind Gert's head.

"Why, Maude," Gert exclaimed, "you worrying about Ellie?"

"Don't think I'd call it worryin," Maude said finally. "Wonderin'. Why'd she never marry, Gert, do ya think?"

Gert cocked her head the way she did when she was going to say something confidential. "Maudie," she asked, "you remember those days, after you and Francis got married? Before Ellie come? You remember how sometimes you'd work so hard, get so much done, you'd feel filled up at the end of the day? Filled up and satisfied?"

"Ye-es." Maude said slowly.

"S'pect Ellie feels that way?" Gert asked.

They stood silently. With an open freezer door, a woman fanned cold air at a cranky toddler in the cart's jump seat. Noticing that they watched, she smiled self-consciously, removed a box of popsicles, and rounded the corner out of sight.

"What'd happen if you didn't move in with Anna?" Maude asked quietly.

Gert shrugged. "She'd lose the farm or marry Byron Kelly, I s'pect."

"Do you need that farm to see you through your old age, Gert?" Maude held her breath at her own breach of etiquette. Gert's finances were none of her business. But she knew Gert knew she wouldn't ask if she didn't need to know.

"'Pends on how long I'm old," Gert said. "Could be I could afford to have her lose the place, if that's what you're gettin' at."

Maude nodded. "I'm thinkin' 'bout sellin' my place," she said softly.

Gert stared. "Sellin'? What in the world? What'd you do if you sold that place?"

"Me?" Maude sounded surprised. "I'd move into the senior citizens, and, well, take it easy."

"And have no one to do for, no one to appreciate the things you still can do. Don't be a fool, Maude Colgan. Ellie stepped in the day Frank died. You ain't had to be alone since you was twenty, and you got no idea how that's keeping you young. You think in a year alone you'd be haulin' that skinny little fanny a yours up outta chairs and into the garden? You think you'd be able to get up those stairs in your house if you didn't do it for a year? And Ellie, what'd Ellie do if you sold that place?"

Maude shrugged. "Get married, I s'pect."

"Oooooh," Gert's voice gentled down again. She reached for another hair pin to re-anchor. "It's that again. Ellie feelin' badly about not being married, Maude?"

"Not exactly," Maude said. "She's actin' strange though, 'n feelin' bad 'cause she ain't feelin' bad 'bout not being married."

Gert's laughter crackled like cereal under milk. "Maudie," she said, turning her cart in the direction of the checkouts, "you remember how hard you cried that day Ellie spit the titty back at you? Not seven months old. That girl's been on her own since."

"Peculiar as hell," Maude grumbled.

"Maybe. But not pitiful."

Maude watched Eleanor back the John Deere up to the hay mower. She crawled off, dropped the pin into the hitch, released the jack, and fitted the power-take-off shaft onto the tractor. Mounting again, she crossed her arms in front, grabbed each side of her T-shirt in her fists, then seemed to reconsider. She wiped the sweat from her face on her shirt sleeve, shifted into gear, and began to move.

Waiting in the garden, Maude started a slow grin. Ellie stepped on the clutch, swiveled in her seat, and looked. Maude leaned against her hoe, her old shirtdress unbuttoned to the waist, its long sleeves brushing her hemline. Ellie stared. Maude nodded, and returned to her work, chuckling as her daughter's laughter gurgled across the field.

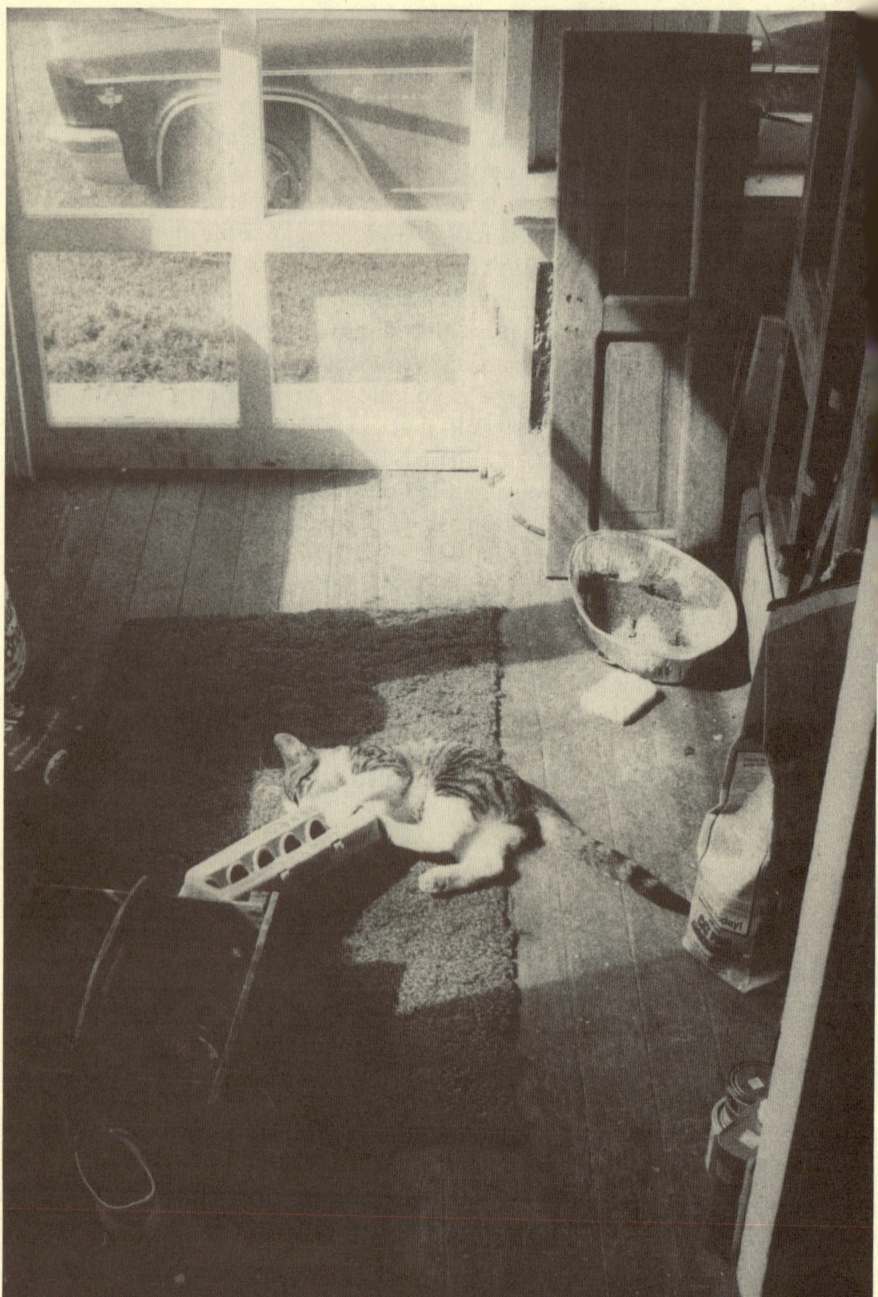

Stray Voltage

A. C. Peters

Marvella tried to remember not to give Mata Hari half-and-half when Al was around. Al liked it all for himself, dumped into the boiled eggshell coffee she made every morning in her gray-speckled coffee kettle. He couldn't face the morning without half-and-half. He needed whitened coffee, he said, to open his day.

"Grows gorilla fur on your chest," he remarked to Jean Ellen one morning. She was visiting their farm near Colwell for two weeks while her parents vacationed in Minnesota. Before he said that, Jean Ellen would have asked to try it. Of course, she knew the part about the fur wasn't true, but she thought the coffee might have some bad effect on a person. She studied her grandpa's face. Most of it was stern and iron-like, but his mouth was clamped to the cup, busily sipping.

Marvella had adopted Mata Hari, the sad-eyed female barn cat, after she was dumped off at the end of their driveway. Now she slunk up to the house twice a day for skimmed milk, or half-and-half when Marvella could spare it, but only when Al was occupied. The cat was cagey. She watched the house from the barn window, waiting for Al to busy himself at something in the yard, maybe fiddle with the Ford half-ton or nip a few branches off a couple of silver maples with the Remington chainsaw. That morning, after Al had lifted the Ford's hood to check the carburetor, Mata Hari shot up the path like a soldier ditching sniper fire to the back door where Marvella waited with the saucer. Marvella petted her while she ate, the little pink tongue lapping with a frenzy, the silky body weaving with the force of hunger to the music her tongue and the cream made together.

"You really ought to get a decent home," she said to the cat.

Turning from the cat, she asked her grandaughter, "Is he still busy with the truck?"

Jean Ellen looked out the window. "Yes, Grandma, he's under the hood. Oh—now he's coming out."

It was time to put Mata Hari outside and she'd hardly had anything but a few licks. Al didn't like to see the cat in the house. He came back to the kitchen after working on the truck and feeding the sheep, a bitten nub of cigar in his mouth.

"The weed whacker was whirring away on top of a hay bale without a care in the world. I haven't used it in days. How do you suppose that happened?" he asked, glancing at his granddaughter. Al sat on the stool behind the kitchen door, loosened his bootlaces and pulled his boots off.

"Maybe a power surge triggered it," Marvella said, setting a bowl of soft-scrambled eggs and a plate of lightly browned baking powder biscuits on the table. Al had once said that her biscuits floated without wings, but now he was becoming forgetful.

"It don't work that way."

"Well, I don't know why not," she said, pouring coffee into their cups. "It seems possible to me." She asked Jean Ellen, "You want milk?"

Al humphed and looked at Jean Ellen, his large dark eyebrows shaped like inverted V's.

"You haven't been playing around down by the barn have you?"

"No, I —"

"Of course she hasn't," Marvella said patiently. "Besides, she hasn't even been here a week."

Al let out an exasperated breath. "What does that have to do—" then he shook his head and sat down at his place at the head of the table. He took a long, slow draw on his coffee and his eyebrows relaxed into two lazy caterpillars lolling on the curve of his forehead. He scooped himself a mound of eggs from the bowl and reached for two biscuits. He had his hand on the strawberry jam when the cat meowed at the back door. Without thinking, Marvella got up to let her in.

"What've you been doing all night?" she asked the cat in a husky, rolling voice, dumping an inch of half-and-half into a cereal bowl and setting it on the cracked linoleum floor. She remembered Al just in time and hid the carton under the sink. He was too busy with his breakfast to notice. Instead he shot her a warning look and said, "Marvella." His eyes moved nervously to Jean Ellen. Sometimes he was afraid of what Marvella would say. His warning was lost on Marvella.

"What?" she said, her hand poised at the end of the cat's tail.

"Nothing," he said, spooning up some jam.

"I think she might be pregnant," Marvella said, stroking the cat's belly. "Maybe she had a fling with one of those handsome toms living in the Phillipson's barn." She tickled the cat under its chin.

"For goodness sake!" Al said. He felt the red creeping up into his face. His mother had always told him that redheads blushed too easily, and he'd always proved her right.

"Well, don't you think she looks pregnant?"

"It's not a topic I would care to discuss at the breakfast table—with the ears of babes listening."

Marvella raised one eyebrow. "For your information, Jean Ellen is no baby. They teach children early in school all about sex, don't they?"

Jean Ellen shrugged and took a bite of egg. She couldn't explain to them all she knew. Even if she'd known what to say, she couldn't get a word in between her Grandpa's steel-belted demeanor and her Grandma's flitting from one thing to another.

Al grabbed the last biscuit and pushed his chair back. "I'm going out to the tool shed," he said, with one hand on the door. He looked down at his stockinged feet and said, "Put the cat out, Jean Ellen. It belongs in the barn."

Marvella took the pink feather duster from the hook behind the door and passed the living room. Her granddaughter rested on the puffy living room couch, with Mata Hari stretched out and settled on top of her back. She had her book opened to a place in the middle and had begun the slow descent, the downward spiral into its pages. Marvella began to dust her plants in the parlor. The strawberry begonias, ferns, and mother-in-law's tongues made scattered green oases, even if the plants were only plastic and silk. She couldn't grow a weed. Her paintings ranged around the white wainscotted walls, giving the parlor a timelessness, like a museum. The room seemed outside of time.

The paintings were real, but in her mind they were all deceptions. The painting of her parents was the picture of deceit, hanging in the corner by the big front window. In it, her mother wore a splashy purple flowered dress and her father looked serious in a dark blue suit. She'd painted it from a snapshot taken on their fiftieth wedding anniversary at the Little Brown Church in Nashua, where they'd been married, and she'd purposely made them both much better-looking than they actually were. Then there was the painting of little Jean Ellen with her nose looking indefinite and smudged, because Marvella couldn't get it to come out right. The rest of her was unmistakably Jean Ellen in a pink seersucker jumpsuit and matching hat. Marvella had painted it when Jean Ellen was almost five. What had happened to that little girl?

The other paintings were landscapes. She'd carefully recreated the farm in each season, fixing such things that needed repair. She'd made the paint job on the house new, and fixed the black, tarred-over patch on the roof. She'd repaired the sloping barn roof, and put an extra blue spruce in front of the house. In that one, the barn and the house, like husband and wife, stood slightly apart with strips of green lawn that resembled arms reaching for each other in the space between them. She painted the birches and weeping willows lining the property fuller and greener. During the years they'd lived on the farm, she'd traced the trees' growth. If they didn't look as healthy as they should have, she had a duty to make them appear beautiful in the paintings. Al had cut down some of the weeping willows because the falling branches were a hazard. She had watched from the front porch as he felled one massive bushy tree after another. They hit the ground with muffled thumps. It took ten minutes, maybe fifteen.

"They passed too quickly after a lifetime of living," she told Al.

"They're a soft wood, Marvella," Al had said. "They don't last forever."

Someone had to fill up the empty spaces. She liked to paint because if she made a mistake on a canvas, she could blot it out or paint over it. She could smooth over a seriously flawed subject until it was nearly perfect. Her latest painting was of Mata Hari sleeping in the bathroom sink in a shaft of sunlight. She looked regal and intelligent. It was Marvella's best work so far, and one she hadn't had to fictionalize.

"Painting is so open to reformation," she told Al once when he asked why she spent so much time upstairs in the bathroom. It was a large bathroom that she'd fixed up as a studio. The light came from the east and south, a pure light, with no shadowy undertones.

"I don't know why you have to go wasting your time on this stuff," he said.

"But look how I can change things." She'd been surprised that he couldn't see the truth of it.

"Marvella, you are sitting up here in the bathroom and the world is running right by you."

"No it's not, it's right here." She'd swept her arms around the room to show him the paintings that dotted the bathroom walls. Maybe it hadn't been the smartest thing to do. He hadn't seemed too impressed. Maybe it was because the paintings in the bathroom were not quite as successful as the ones in the parlor. Some of them were odd: a squirrel with crazed, rabid-looking eyes; a tree that had somehow dried the wrong color—leaves an unnatural pastel aqua. Her first attempt at painting a figure: Ray, her brother, looking startled, as if she'd rolled him out like dough, froze him, then slathered him on the canvas like a strip of wallpaper. He'd had a crewcut and his hair stood on end. But even these paintings were efforts, worth something if you considered artistic development.

"You're living in a dream world," Al said, shaking his head.

She became irritated. After all, painting was work. It wasn't as if she could slip up to the bathroom for ten minutes, throw a few dabs of paint on the canvas, and call it finished. It took time and engineering to do what she did. Al was not capable of understanding her art. Maybe he just couldn't understand her.

"Someday I'll paint my masterpiece and you might not be in it," she said, crossing her arms over her ample chest. "How would you feel about that?"

"I guess I'd have to live with it, Marvella," he said, coolly flicking his cigar out of his shirt pocket and sticking it in the corner of his mouth. Then Al had gone out to the shed and Marvella had heard the tractor engine sputter. He rode right by the window—that was why Al liked the John Deere so much. You had to look up to him when he was in the seat. He'd glanced toward the bathroom window at Marvella and turned his eyes away, pretending he hadn't seen her.

That's just it, she thought, people see us only as we appear, like two plump, happy-go-lucky grapes snug in a lime jello. But look at us. And jello is appropriate, she thought. It's cold inside. Once it warms up, it's soup. She was so upset she called her sister

Violet, who could sometimes make her feel like life was a smooth road, or a length of satin and that she was traveling along it, or sewing like a machine slipping out endless stitches, with no cares. Flying down the road at sixty-five miles an hour, sewing one long seam. It had been a long time since she'd felt that way.

"How do we look to you, really, Al and me, not just from the outside?" she'd asked Violet. "Do we appear to go together?"

"Of course you go together, Marvella, you've been married for, what, going on thirty-five years now. Why wouldn't you?" Violet said.

"It's not that easy. Sometimes I think he's somebody else disguised to look like Al, like it's all a trick."

"You've had another argument. It'll all blow over by tomorrow. Doesn't it always?"

Violet tapped something on the counter. It sounded metered, like the tick of a clock. Marvella imagined her sister's pale fingers, the nail tips perfectly rounded and impatient to be off doing something important, like practicing for the typing classes she'd started. Violet had her eye on the receptionist's job at the clinic in New Hampton.

"It might blow over, it might not. What I'm saying, Violet, is it might blow over and over but it never sinks in, you know what I mean?"

"Well, not exactly," Violet said. "Can I call you back? I've got something in the oven." She hung up.

Marvella set the phone in its cradle. She still had things she wanted to say. She reached down and picked up the cat.

"You're the only one who'll talk to me today," she said, scratching Mata Hari in the sensitive spot under her chin. The cat was intelligent. Sometimes when Marvella was concentrating on doing her best job painting, Mata Hari would jump up onto the counter near the easel and watch. Yesterday afternoon she was working out a new painting of Al and her from a twenty-year-old photograph—Al had fuzzy red sideburns and his hair flopped over onto his collar. Marvella was much less matronly, her eyelids tighter, her stomach firmer. Al wore a white T-shirt and jeans in the picture. You wouldn't catch him wearing them now. Denim overalls; he had seven pairs, more than a few of them nearly worn clean through the seat and soft as skin.

In the painting, she'd captured their young bodies. Her figures were improving, but when it came to faces, she couldn't always trust herself to paint the truth. She scraped off the beginning of Al's face. It seemed to be a likeness of someone else. She didn't recognize him. She'd have to start over. She rubbed the canvas with a rag. Mata Hari blinked at Marvella and meowed. "Why?" or perhaps it was "How?" it sounded like to Marvella, although she wasn't sure what it meant.

Perhaps the problem with Al's face lay with the skin-tone color. Marvella couldn't remember whether cats saw in color or black and white. She grabbed a square of paper and smoothed on some of the tint she'd just scraped off. Mata Hari watched her hands as she mixed more paint on another square of paper, increasing the yellow tone. Marvella set both of the papers on the counter and watched to see what the cat would do.

"Smarty-cat," she said, running her hand down the length of brown fur. It crackled with static electricity. Mata Hari raised her head to Marvella, imploring her with sad green eyes.

"Well, what do you think?" she asked the cat, then glanced at the bathroom door to be sure Al wasn't spying on her. She didn't need him walking in just now. She was only experimenting, and Al took things too seriously most of the time. Mata Hari sniffed both blobs of paint, arched her back and feigned an attack pose. Her paw straightened and she batted at one of the squares. Marvella smiled. It was the one with the added yellow tone. "Would have tried it anyway," she said, mixing more paint to match.

The Ortloffs had invited them to go out to Red's Supper Club, a restaurant outside of Mason City that served mainly red meats and pale vegetables. Jean Ellen said she was old enough to stay alone.

"Well, all right," Marvella said from the bedroom, where she was putting on her pantyhose, "but I'll write the number down just to be sure. You just call me if there's anything."

"I stay home alone all the time," Jean Ellen said. She had a red licorice twist dangling from her mouth, so it sounded more like, "I sfay home alom ul de sime."

"What did she say?" Al asked. "Is she sick?"

Marvella rolled her eyes and said, "She said she stays home alone all the time."

"I don't doubt it," Al said, snapping the lid on his Aqua Velva aftershave, setting it back on the dresser. He rummaged around in the back of the closet. "Marvella, have you been storing paint in here?"

"Not that I remember," she said. She had squeezed into her blue chemise, the one that Al had long ago claimed made her eyes look like the water off Catalina, where they'd gone on their honeymoon.

"My good shoes have orange paint on them," Al said, bringing them out into the light for closer examination. "Looks sort of like cat paws." He turned one of the shoes away from the glare of the light.

She peered at the shoes. It dawned on Marvella then that the orange cat paws were the same color as the yellow-tinted skin tones she'd mixed up that afternoon. Mata Hari must have gone from the bathroom studio directly to Al's shoes.

"Yes," she said, "I did store a few tubes of paint in there. Must have dripped." She whisked the shoes away from Al before he had time to look at them again. "I'll take care of these. Wear your black ones."

She marched into the kitchen and hid the shoes under the sink. They would clean up just as easily tomorrow. When Al came out of the bedroom in his black shoes and his dark blue sports jacket, she turned around for him to notice the dress. He gave the two cigars he was tucking into his shirt pocket his rapt attention.

"Aren't you going to say anything?" she asked.

"What am I supposed to say?"

"About my eyes?"

Al nodded. "Did you go for your check-up or something?"

"It's more like something," she said. Well, what did it matter if he thought of her in the old way or not? Tonight she would let go, have fun. She didn't care. She picked up her white summer bag from the kitchen table and brushed by him to peek in on Jean Ellen who sprawled on the parlor couch with a book. The girl read. She knew the meanings of words Marvella had never heard of; she referred to Al as "pertinacious" when it came to the cat, and the cat as "expeditious" when it came to hiding from Al. Marvella had looked up both words. Jean Ellen had a vocabulary.

"Be good," Marvella told her. "Call us." She pecked Jean Ellen on the cheek and felt like it was twenty-two years ago, and she was talking to her adolescent daughter, Katie.

"I'll be fine," Jean Ellen said, the cat snuggling next to her stomach.

Al and Marvella got in the car and drove in silence the five miles to the Ortloff's. Gravel plinked against the car. There was nothing to say.

The Ortloffs farmed pigs. You could smell it in the kitchen and on their clothes, the unmistakable sweetish scent of hog manure. Patti tried to cover it up with Exclamation! perfume, but the smell seeped through her pores. Marvella was used to it. Robert did nothing to cover it up. Hogs were his life's work.

They had known the Ortloffs for more than twenty years. Tonight they were all going for Red's special: barbecued pork chops. Those over fifty-five got a dollar off anything on the menu. The restaurant called it the senior special. Although Robert had the most successful farming operation in Chickasaw County, he pinched pennies.

"Hey-ho, buddy," Robert said, slapping Al's shoulder.

"Did you make the reservations?" Al asked. He was in a sour mood.

"Sure thing." Robert let the snub roll away into the thick air.

Tonight was Al and Marvella's turn to drive. When they'd all settled into the Buick, Marvella and Patti in the back, the men in front, Robert turned his head and peered over the seat.

"We're eating high on the hog tonight," he said, his face as expressionless as a bag of feed. He liked pig jokes.

"Pork chops don't sound all that good to me," Patti said, speaking to Marvella.

"Glad the people running the grocery stores don't go by that philosophy," Robert said. He hummed a tuneless song in a weak voice, skipping notes when the car ran over bumps in the road.

Al reached over and switched on the radio. Robert's humming burned through his nerves.

"Wouldn't it be quicker to take the back way?" Marvella asked Al. When she drove, she always took the shortest route. She rarely arrived on time, though, because there was just so much to see. Still, it comforted her to find shortcuts. Checking the map before she took any trip made her feel organized.

"We'll take care of the driving," Al said, peering at her in the rear view mirror. "You girls just hold on tight." He sped up to show off. The hulking silhouettes of roadside trees streaked by the windows. Bugs and moths flew through the two gauzy ribbons thrown by the Buick's headlights.

Marvella glanced over at Patti and rolled her eyes.

"How's that cat of yours?" Patti asked.

"She's surviving."

"If she doesn't work out, you know, she can always come live in our barn. We can always use a few more cats."

"Oh no," Marvella half-whispered, "I couldn't. Mata Hari is like member of the family."

"A moocher," Al chimed in from the front.

"I know a good spot for a cat like that," Robert said, no doubt referring to the previous winter when one of his cats was hit on the road in front of their house. He had nailed it—frozen, standing up—to the post at the end of their driveway. Patti had sneaked down one evening with a claw hammer and pried it off. She told Marvella later that it had made her sick to her stomach. Marvella wanted to ask her which part it was that made her sick, prying it off, or having it there in the first place, but she didn't want to dredge it up.

"The be-kind-to-animals-people will hunt you down with cattle prods if you ever do that again," Patti said.

"Good for you," Marvella mouthed at her.

When they arrived at Red's, their waitress, a middle-aged woman with bottle-black hair and a name tag that read Sylvia, told them that her name was Sylvia and that the restaurant was out of pork chops.

"Well then," Robert said, "we still get the dollar off, right?"

"Only if you're over fifty-five," Sylvia said. "You're certainly not that old."

Al sat up straighter in his chair and sucked in his stomach. Patti rolled her eyes and pretended to look for something in her purse.

Robert smiled. "I'm a grandfather twice now."

"Well, you sure fooled me," she said, smiling widely, whipping out her pad and pen to take their orders. When she swayed back to the kitchen, she peeked over her shoulder at them before pushing open the door.

Patti leaned over to Marvella, and whispered, "Some people will do anything for a tip."

They ordered beef steak with baked potatoes drizzled with melted butter, accompanied by small plates of lettuce with French dressing trailed across the top.

After their dinner, Al and Robert both insisted on paying for the meal. They stood at the counter, their bodies weaving from their two gin sours. They were gazing cow-eyed at one another as though they felt sentimental. Al, who was taller than Robert by at least half a foot, rested his hand on Robert's shoulder. Robert gazed up at him as though Al was his older brother.

"Listen pal," Robert said too loudly. "I gotta use the Mastercard or I'll have to start paying a fee on it."

"Bobby," Al said, "it's our turn for this one. You paid last time."

Sylvia smiled patiently behind the cash register, wringing her hands at the waist of her ruffle-edged black apron, one hip flung out.

"No, no, no, no. Last time was at the Pub, remember? You paid."

"We dutched it, Bobby. All I know is, I'm getting it this time."

"Buddy boy, I don't use the card and I'm sunk, you know?"

Marvella got up, felt herself sway slightly, and hurried over to them, her purse banging against her thigh. Patti followed. Marvella felt steady. She was not drunk or even high from the drink. Her blood pressure had just dropped when she'd gotten up too fast from the table.

"I've got an idea," she said. "Let me pay this time. It'll go so much quicker."

Sylvia rocked back on her heels with that one.

"I don't know . . ." Al said.

"Then we can leave," Marvella said.

Sylvia seemed to agree to this, because she opened the cash register with a ding.

"Sweetie," whispered Al, "but you never pay."

"If she pays, then I drive home," Patti said, winking at Marvella.

"Well!" Robert said, his mouth dropping open.

"Then it's settled," Marvella said. She slipped her checkbook from her purse and signed her name before they could talk her out of it.

Patti got behind the wheel and Marvella sat in the passenger seat. The two men climbed in and pushed their knees into the backs of the vinyl seats. "I'm taking the shortcut," Patti said. Robert snorted.

It felt odd to have Patti driving the Buick. Marvella herself rarely drove; she let Al drive. He preferred it that way. The car seemed like Al's toy. Marvella thought that they were all riding inside Al's hollowed-out toy elephant, an elephant with a smooth gait and contour seats and new Goodyear tires.

"This is the life," Robert said, leaning back and putting his hands on the soft gray velvet upholstery.

Al sat straight and stiff. He didn't like anyone else playing with his toys. Patti drove faster, and Marvella remembered the senior special. "I don't think the waitress gave us our discount."

"Are you sure?" asked Patti, pressing harder on the gas pedal. The car leaped forward and crossed the yellow center line.

Al made a strangled noise.

"Turn around," Robert slurred. "I left her a tip."

Patti paid no attention. Her eyes were on the road.

Robert sat up and leaned close to Patti's ear. "I said turn around," he hissed. The veins in his forehead looked ready to explode.

"For godsakes, Robert," Al said. "It's only four dollars." When he laid a brotherly hand on Robert's shoulder, Robert looked at it as though it were wet cement. Al took his hand away.

"It's okay, Robert," Marvella said, turning around in the seat so she could look him in the eye. "We're going home. It was my money anyway." It came out more sharply than she'd intended. She shifted back in her seat. Afterwards, she thought she should say she was sorry or make some joke, but she watched the road and kept quiet.

Robert sat back against the seat. He was quiet the rest of the way home. At the hog farm, the headlights flashed on Patti and Robert's white Rambler and the aluminum siding of the buildings behind it.

After they'd dropped Patti and Robert off, Al loosened up. He looped one arm over the steering wheel and reached the other arm behind her. She felt blanketed, protected like some rare, caged bird.

"You sure put a cork in Robert," he said, and turned to study her. It was the same curious, fascinated gaze he had for her that night on Catalina Island.

"He had a point about the senior special," Marvella said. "It hardly pays to get old anymore."

Al smiled and curled his arm, pulling Marvella next to him, nuzzling his lips on her forehead. She snuggled close to the smooth polyester of his sport coat. He smelled faintly of damp leaves and fall, her favorite season.

"Someone's been out in my truck," Al said in the kitchen the next morning. "The radio was playing and the window was cracked open three inches." With his eyes, he tried to coax Jean Ellen into looking up at him.

"I'm sure there's some reason—" Marvella said.

"Well, I'm sure there is, too," Al said. "Jean Ellen?" He noticed Mata Hari lounging on the braided kitchen rug. "What's that cat doing in here?"

"I didn't do it," Jean Ellen said, picking the cat up and taking it into the parlor.

"I'm sure you didn't, sweetie," Marvella called after her. "That truck is a wreck anyway. The radio probably has a short in it. Right, Al?"

"There's nothing wrong with the truck."

"You're always out there fixing it," Marvella reminded him.

"The radio's okay." He stamped out the door, letting the screen door slam. Green paint flakes drifted to the sill.

"He's testy in the morning," she called to Jean Ellen. "It'll all be fine after lunch."

Jean Ellen appeared again in the doorway holding the cat. "Mata Hari could come live with us," she said. "Mom wouldn't care. She'd be good company for me." Jean Ellen sounded like Marvella's daughter, Katie, when she was young.

She looked at the girl's thin face, the haunting cheekbones jutting out, the straight, serious mouth, the thick eyebrows. Eyebrows inherited from her grandfather, Marvella thought. Katie and Roger left the girl too much on her own. Maybe it was true that Jean Ellen lacked company, or supervision. But maybe she didn't need the supervision. Katie and Roger often went on these trips. No children allowed, Roger said. Their home might be as cold as an iron bed frame, but if she allowed Jean Ellen to take Mata Hari, she would have no one left in the house to talk to. It was not that the cat was everything to her, but she could talk to it. Strange that an animal could come to mean so much.

"I'll think about it," she finally said, swallowing the hard knot that had formed in her throat. Jean Ellen would be with them for three more days.

Jean Ellen blinked at Marvella. She had Katie's brown eyes. Marvella fell into them. She had a hard time climbing back out. "Of course you can take her," Marvella said. Jean Ellen jumped up, hugged the cat, then hugged Marvella. She forgot the cat until it scrabbled its claws against the cloth of her shirt. "Oh honey, honey," Marvella said, giggling like a girl, not sure whether she spoke to Jean Ellen or the cat.

The painting of the two of them was coming along. Marvella had gotten the faces just about right. Her own chin looked longer than it should have, but it looked better than her real chin so she'd kept it. The background, their gardens lush with half-finished flower beds, needed to be completed, but she wasn't in any hurry. She was judging the color of Al's hair. She thought Al might be pleased by the gracious amount of red hair she had put on his head. Mata Hari sat at the sink waiting for a drink of water. Was the hair too orange? She wasn't sure. Hair color was at least as complex as skin tones.

"Just a minute," she said to the cat, and turned to compare the color of her own hair in the painting with Al's. The colors were close, closer than in real life. Al creaked up the stairs to the studio. He had on a tattered old pair of overalls and a Northrup King seed corn cap. He started saying something about the fuse box in the basement, then stopped. He stared at the painting.

"Say, that's us." He bent closer to the canvas. "Isn't it?"

"A long time ago." It sounded wistful. It made her a little sad to be saying that, but she pushed the feeling away and brushed back the strands of steel-colored hair that had fallen onto her forehead.

"Now, now," he said, carefully. "It wasn't all that long ago, was it?" He seemed to be figuring the years, the wrinkles deepening between his eyes. "You still look the same." He put his hand in the middle of her back. It was warm there, like a small fire, catching and growing.

"You're not wearing your glasses," she said, but she was pleased at what he'd said. Even if he hadn't been sincere.

"Always a reason for everything I do, Marvella."

She had to laugh, and so did he. They giggled in front of the fiction of themselves until Marvella accidentally brushed up against the wet paint and got some blue on her hip. She turned to the sink for her damp rag. Mata Hari was on the counter batting her paw at the water faucet. She hit at the stainless steel faucet—her paw resembling a fur covered, thin brown stick—until the water gushed out of the tap. Then she leaned out over the precipice of cultured marble sink and stuck out her pink tongue.

She scooped in tonguefuls of cool water, ignoring everything around her but the rushing water. Marvella and Al just watched, and everything came together as Mata Hari licked and licked. I'll bet she knows we're watching her, Marvella thought. Show-off. She glanced at Al and saw that Mata Hari's action had not been lost on him.

"I suppose she turns on light switches, too," Al said, as if from far away. "And radios; the whole ball of wax." He pulled a fresh, unwrapped cigar from his pocket, zipped it open, and stuck it in the corner of his mouth.

Marvella nodded, then shook her head. "Probably not. How could she? She's only a cat. You can't blame her for everything." She knew Mata Hari hadn't turned on the electrical tools and light switches and truck radios. Al had. Mata Hari could only get a drink and flush the toilet. Marvella didn't want to say anything, but Al was becoming absent-minded.

"The cat's got to go," Al said. "This can't go on. We'd be asking for trouble. Our electric's already too high without this." He reached forward, stretching to pick Mata Hari up by the scruff of the neck.

Marvella stepped in front of him, blocking him from the cat. "I have something to say about that, too."

Al's cigar perked up at the corner of his mouth, his eyes burned. Marvella put her hands on her hips. Al let the breath out fast through his nose, moved his mouth as though he was going to speak, then turned and stomped down the stairs. Marvella touched the soft, sparse fur on the bridge of Mata Hari's nose. She heard the screen door slam downstairs. As she ran her hand down the cat's back, she heard the truck start up and pull away fast from the yard. When she looked out the window, dust spun up the driveway and Al was gone.

She went down to the kitchen to fix herself a pot of coffee. Jean Ellen, her clothes rumpled, hair sticking up, came out of the parlor with an open paperback in one hand. Marvella glanced at the cover. Jean Ellen was reading *Fanny Hill*.

"What's the matter with Grandpa?"

Marvella tried to pull her mouth into a half smile. "He's just nervous."

"About his radio?"

"Yes, that and a few other things."

Jean Ellen wrinkled her nose. "Smells rotten in here."

Marvella sniffed. There was a thin, sharp smell near the cupboards. It wasn't the smell of a dead mouse. It was more a blending of hidden smells, crowded together like fear. Jean Ellen had her eyes in the book again, reading as she glided through the kitchen on automatic pilot and beyond the parlor door. Marvella sniffed at the wood along the cupboards. She remembered that she had stashed things in them, things that were embarrassing or inconvenient, like the carton of half-and-half she'd shoved in the other morning. She opened the door and saw the toes of Al's good shoes pointing at her, with Mata Hari's prints dried on.

After the incident with Al, Mata Hari disappeared. She was too sensitive, Marvella believed, to put up with the disagreeable atmosphere in the house. Marvella and Jean Ellen searched for her all afternoon in the woodlot and in the barn. The next day Marvella even called the Phillipsons and asked them to check their outbuildings.

"Mata who?" Gert Phillipson asked over the phone in a thin exasperated voice, as if Marvella was foolish. Cats were of no interest to Gert.

Jean Ellen hadn't picked up a book that morning. She'd spent the morning and afternoon searching the woods behind the tool shed.

"She doesn't need all those words, anyway," said Al. He had come in for an afternoon coffee break, and stood just inside the door with his cup, so he didn't have to unlace his boots. "It puts ideas into her head."

Marvella sniffed. "Better ideas than empty," she said, looking at Al until he turned away, his face red. "Do you know where the cat is?" she asked, staring at his back.

"What do you mean?" Al turned around, his forehead crinkling up, then flattening out, his eyes burning into hers. His face grew redder. "I don't like the cat, but I wouldn't have done anything."

She began to close the cupboard doors, wipe up the counter with a dishrag, keeping an eye on him. "I thought you might have taken it somewhere out of the way."

Al let out a long breath, set his cup down, and fumbled in his pocket for a cigar. "Everything's got to be a drama with you, doesn't it? I wouldn't have hurt the cat if that's what you think. You sit up in the bathroom painting all day and you don't even see what's happening in your own life." He reached for the door knob.

Marvella knew the signs. He was going to stomp off again. He was going to climb up onto the John Deere and joy ride around the hay fields. He was going to sit above the world and leave her back holding up its weight.

"What's going on," Marvella said, "is that the cat's missing and Jean Ellen is out in the woods crying against a tree trunk." Al sighed and pulled his hand from the door knob. His eyes considered something on the floor Marvella could not see. He shook his head, and his eyes met Marvella's, slow like trickling water. "You care about that cat more than . . . anything," he said, gripping the cigar between his teeth.

"She listens to me," Marvella said, looking steadily at him.

"I'll find the damn thing then," he said. He took his cigar out of his mouth and stuffed it into his overalls. He turned to leave, then faced her again. His voice was almost a whisper. "What do you tell her that you can't say to me?"

"Well." She looked into his eyes. "Secrets. I tell her secrets about our past lives. I tell her about when you had more hair on your head than you knew what to do with. About how you and me used to put the kids to bed, turn the record player on low, and dance in the kitchen in our socks. She wants to hear it all."

"I do too," he said softly. "I want to hear it all, too."

He stood in front of her like such a little boy, and a man, too. That gruff stone fell away, and then there was nothing in between them. They stood close enough that she could reach and touch his hair.

Posings

Lisa A. Phillips

In the time of the posings, my sister Shirley was almost due. At eight months and three weeks, her belly was tremendous. You could practically smell that child inside of her, filled out and warm in its chamber of fluid, silent now but poised to emerge with a squawk so mighty we'd never dare forsake it. When Shirley stood under the glare of the studio lights, her spine a burdened, backwards c, she did not hide her fatigue. "If you're going to take so many pictures, at least let me sit down," she snapped.

Alyson Quinn hesitated. I could see it on her face; sitting down was not what she had planned for Shirley or for any of us. She wanted us to pose one at a time standing backed up against the grey barn wall. Aside from that, we could slouch or pout or grin however we pleased. As Alyson surveyed my sister through her camera lens, I dragged the metal folding chair I'd been sitting in across the wooden slatted floor over to Shirley. Drawing back from the tripod, Alyson frowned.

"Thanks, Monona," Shirley said and dropped into the chair. Furrowing her brows, she rubbed her legs and feet. "They itch like screwing in the hay." Alyson laughed, surprised and pleased to be let in on this bawdy quip. The chair creaked as Shirley leaned back, cocked her head, and spread her legs to balance the weight of her womb. She looked like a disgruntled adolescent waiting for dinner. Her dangling wrists grazed the rough lumber of the wall in back of the chair.

I thought my sister brave, letting her picture be taken by anyone but family while she was in this uncomfortable, swollen state. Of course I did not know what Alyson was planning for Shirley. I did not know how Alyson would frame her subject, what the angle would be. Would Shirley be dwarfed, a distant, misshapen figure in the expanse of barn wall, or would the lens zoom her in so close you could see the razor stubble like pepper on her shins? The tiny hole in the shoulder of her faded red maternity T-shirt?

Alyson shot a couple of dozen pictures, several times adjusting her aperture and light meter or the slant of the studio lights. Without a chair to keep still in, I paced the edge of the scene, taking care not to step inside the range of the lens. I studied Shirley anxiously. Her face was beginning to glow red and moist from the heat.

"You almost done?" I asked. Alyson didn't answer. She just held up her hand to silence me. But it wasn't too many more shots before the posing was over.

"That will do," Alyson said. I hastily stepped in front of the camera to help Shirley rise, grabbing her damp hand and tugging her watery weight upward.

Alyson walked us to the door. "When are you due?"

"September twenty-ninth," I said.

Alyson looked directly at Shirley. "Thank you so much for coming in. Especially so close to your time," Alyson said. She ran her palm up and down the door frame and her eyes flickered over us. Then she leaned against the frame, extending her hand to shake our hands. "Thanks again," she said and smiled, looking content.

"Good luck with this project," Shirley said. Her stomach nearly touched Alyson's. "I don't exactly know if I want to see what I look like now, but that's how it goes," she shrugged.

"Good-bye," I said and turned my face into the sharp glare of the sun. Certain that Alyson was still watching us, I held onto Shirley's leather-dry elbow as we left the barn, stepping into a heat that smelled like old wine.

Shirley did not need me and resisted my touch until she realized I was gripping her so tightly that pulling away would look like a dispute. "You'd think I was headed for Friendship Hall, the way you're escorting me," she muttered. Friendship Hall was the fifteen-room old age home on the south end of Ox Bend. In front of the grim brick building was a yellow marquee, topped with blinking red, green, and blue light bulbs. The message in black capital letters said, "Come visit us. Love is never old."

Shirley lit a cigarette. The smoke cut into the heady odor of the outdoors. We walked away from Alyson's studio on the dead end half-moon on Second Street West.

"Alyson's different, huh?" Shirley sighed.

"I don't know why we're so interesting to her," I said.

"Look, she's from, where, Chicago? Grew up with subway trains and tall buildings. She's in the middle of her own *National Geographic* special here in Iowa," Shirley said.

"I never thought we'd rank right up there with the Pygmies."

"She's okay, Monona. I liked what she said in the paper." I remembered reading the passage to Shirley. She was in bed, struggling with the morning nausea of her first term, and I read her the town's weekly, *The Trumpeter*. There was an article about Alyson. She said she loved photography because she was drawn to the "human intensity revealed" in her subjects. Shirley sat up and said, "There's something. Human intensity revealed." Then she flopped back on the bed, holding her stomach. I was a little surprised. Shirley was rarely attracted to anything poetic.

She and I stopped in town at the Ideal Cafe for coffee and air-conditioning. "Are you scared?" I asked, once she'd eased herself into the booth.

"Of what, Monona?"

"Of birthing."

"I try not to think about it. They say it's as bad as having a kidney stone, and I saw Marshall gutted down with one of those. It hurt just to look at him wriggling on the floor like that." She sipped her coffee, winced, and asked the waitress to bring her a tall glass of ice. "It's too hot for hot drinks," she explained.

"Maybe what's more scary is bringing kids up. You never know how they will turn out," I said awkwardly. How could I imagine? No baby was in my belly. No baby had ever been and, as I was still single, I hadn't tried for one either. But this matter—of how children turn out—had always concerned me. Every time I read in the newspaper about a murder, I thought, that killer was once a curled-up embryo in some mother. How could people be so defective, busting themselves out of gear like some lemon of an automobile?

"Twenty years from now we'll just have to meet right here to talk about it," Shirley said. She poured a container of creamer into her now-iced coffee. The stream darkened and billowed like storm clouds over the cubes.

On my farm, twenty years would bring a few new pieces of machinery, perhaps a few more acres if the Larsons next door ever sold their land, and still uncertain profits. Probably we'd have a summer not too unlike this one, with days made long with a somnolent heat that crept into the corners and back rooms of even the best-cooled homes. Shirley and I would be floating through middle age. She'd probably still be hinting that I should get out of the tractor seat to pursue a more feminine profession. She'd be catching her breath from two decades of growing her first child and maybe others. This child she carried inside her now would be working or in college, hopefully good for something and making her proud.

"Twenty years from now we can look back on a set of professional black and white photos of everybody and their brothers," I said.

"I'll have a reminder of how I looked pregnant with my first." Shirley downed the last of her glass and sighed. I could smell her breath faintly, stained with the decaying odors of coffee and the cigarette.

It was easier to imagine two months from now, when Shirley's child would suckle at her breast in an innocent time of dependence and nurturing, before the development of personality, or profession. I looked forward to taking my turns with the baby during the winter, when there was little to do on the farm and Shirley needed a break. I would be a good balancing force to Shirley and Marshall's ways. They would be fine parents, but they had their cigarettes and their swearing, their disdain for education past high school.

I held the heavy glass door of the cafe open for Shirley to angle herself through. On the sidewalk, she hung her elbow over my shoulder. "You'll have one, too, little sister. You're a big, tough farmer now but I remember when we were girls. You told me in all your little woman seriousness that our babies had already started to grow inside of us. They wouldn't be ready to come out for many years, but they'd already been planted by God. One or two or three in every girl. You said you hoped we'd have ours together."

"I guess I'd better hurry up," I said.

"No joke, you'd better. I hear it's Ladies Night at the Top Hat tonight." We laughed and started back to her apartment, ambling together through the heat, her belly stuck out in front of us like a trophy we'd just won, unwieldy and fantastic.

Alyson Quinn had lived and worked in her studio on Second Street West for about seven years. She'd moved in when she was in graduate school at the university thirty miles east of us, the place where I'd gotten my ag science degree three years ago. Now she was teaching there, an assistant professor of Graphic Arts and Photography.

We never thought she'd stay in town for long. At first, every time we saw her load up the back of her beige Ford station wagon with boxes and rectangular packages wrapped in brown mailing paper, we believed that was the end of her residency in Ox Bend. But then we'd see her a day or two later in the drugstore or the post office. She'd mention an exhibition or a new class she was teaching, and we knew the packages had nothing to do with moving and everything to do with the demands of her profession.

So we watched her, and wondered what she did to amuse herself, living solo in her rickety two-story house. We saw her shoveling snow off her driveway in the winter, clad in black, steel-toed boots and a trench coat, a Santa Claus-red wool scarf as wide as a shawl wrapped around her neck. She smiled at everyone in town with naive, arduous verve. Her teeth were large and set close together, crowding her mouth. She had olive-tan skin and a long nose and was darker than anyone in town. Everyone wondered whether she was Italian or Spanish, and we smiled back with only half the effort. We were mildly suspicious of her. So few strangers moved into town. Alyson's Ox Bend citizenship was too purposeful. Until the time of the posings, we had no idea what this purpose might be.

It took the people of Ox Bend some time to agree to be photographed. Last February, Alyson announced her intention to capture the town and its two-hundred-and-ten or so residents on film. She would exhibit the photographs in town and call it the "Ox Bend Project." She publicized her plans enthusiastically. She got that article written in *The Trumpeter*. She spoke at churches, the Rotary Club, the Women of the Moose, PTA meetings. She made signs with a number to call for an appointment to pose, and a map to her studio, and posted them in the laundromat, the post office, the town clerk's office, and Casey's. But no one went to pose. It wasn't clear why she would want to do this project and why we should participate. We all saw each other regularly, and had plenty of photographs, with albums of births, weddings, summer picnics, and graduation parties stacked on our coffee tables.

Despite this response, Alyson began to hold open house hours at her studio. Every Monday, Wednesday, and Friday from 3:30 to 8:30 p.m., you could drop in and pose without an appointment. You could pose on impulse, on your way home from the store or the office. But March and April passed and no one, as far as anyone knew, had stopped by. I imagined Alyson diligently standing on guard during the open house hours. She probably spent her time grading student work from an Introduction to Photography course, studying slightly blurred images of panting dogs, the latticed undersides of bridges, a slim, naked back, a painfully contrived set-up of a banana on the seat of a Honda moped. When I was at the university, I'd seen this kind of effort. The work of student artists hung in the student union, the library, and some dorm rooms I'd been in. It was clear how little of it was any good. I felt sorry for Alyson. Surely it pained her to see so much half-baked work.

The situation changed for Alyson when Bill Hussman died. One July evening, he'd tried to race a freight train across a stretch of tracks in south Minneapolis, but his old Buick stalled. I hadn't seen Bill for years. He'd joined the Navy after high school, then moved to the Twin Cities to work construction jobs. Most of Bill's family lived in Ox Bend or elsewhere in southeast Iowa, so he was sent back here to be mourned and buried.

After the funeral, everyone gathered at the VFW lodge for coffee. Bill's older brother Jack and five of his friends stacked up six packs of Bud Lite on the table and began to drink. Jack had been in the Navy, too. He worked for eight years on what he described as dangerous intelligence missions. Whenever Jack came home on leave, he went drinking nightly and dealt out his final good-byes as if they were playing cards. He swore each time he'd be dead before his next leave. But Jack got out of the service alive. It was Bill who ended up dying young and far away from any Naval base.

"They never made him risk his neck," Jack blurted out loudly in the echoing social hall of the VFW lodge, pulling a Bud from their seventh six-pack. "That was the problem. His whimpy Navy filing clerk job never gave him a whiff of death so he never learned what it smelled like. With me, I sniff it ten miles away. A hundred miles away. Ox Bend is lucky to have me. I'll tell them when danger's coming." It began to rain outside. The lodge grew humid and the odor of beer bloomed hot and sour around him and his buddies.

Then Jack stuffed his handkerchief up the sleeve of his black suit and stood up, wavering on his feet. "Where's that photographer? We need some funeral pictures, classy ones." Jack marched through the rain to Alyson's studio, bringing his five friends with him. Alyson was not at the funeral. I imagined she was more than ready for them.

And with his posing, Jack broke the rest of the town's reluctance. It was as if a tribal elder had gravely nodded permission for us to proceed. The town slowly began to filter through

Alyson's studio. First, the rest of the VFW members arrived in her converted barn. They told their wives and their children to go, too, even though the kids complained that they'd already done this at the beginning of the school year for class pictures. Then friends of the wives came, curious about what they'd look like in black and white. Dreaming of old Bette Davis stills, they coated their eyelashes in layers of mascara. They, in turn, brought their husbands and children along.

Details of the project were passed around town from those who'd posed. After Alyson developed the photos, she planned to exhibit them in the VFW Lodge. She said she'd advertise the show in *The Des Moines Register*. People were happy about the prospect of tourism, something the town had never attracted before. Some thought the city council would even want to think about a legal contract with Alyson because she might profit if admission were charged, or if she sold any of her work to visitors. Meanwhile, Alyson herself was more visible. Families who'd posed and decided she wasn't so strange after all invited her for dinner at the Ideal or in their homes. They said that she was very gracious, though a little dreamy and oddly-dressed.

The younger married couples and singles were the most reluctant to pose for Alyson. Out drinking at the Ox Bend Tap, they mocked the project, wondering out loud why it was so important to get everyone's ugly faces on film. But then their parents urged them to pose the same way they urged them to show up in church on Sunday mornings. "It's important to have a full set," the parents explained. Their children relented, deciding a few minutes' worth of posing wasn't worth arguing about. Once they knew they were going, they prepared carefully. I saw them on their way to the studio. The men shaved close and splashed on cologne, as if scent could matter in a photograph. The women wore their newest jeans and silky blouses, unbuttoned to just above the clasps of their bras. Before this last trimester of her pregnancy, Shirley would have looked as fine as any of them. But she couldn't see the use of trying hard. Her belly would dominate the photograph no matter what she wore.

I went back to Alyson's a couple of days after Shirley's posing. I'd been walking the rows of corn and had picked a few ears to bring to the elevator for a moisture check. I was pretty sure the corn was ready for harvest. For a while it looked like a tough growing season. A wet spring delayed planting a little longer than we were comfortable with, but after that, the season was fine and held few surprises. Prices would be up a little, and I'd be pulling in an average yield I could get out of the ground by Halloween.

I was proud at the sight of the tall, dry brown stalks. This time around my father had let me do it all—the negotiations with the bank, the seed buying, the planting, the cultivating, and now the harvesting. I'd be hauling the beans and corn to the elevator as my sister nursed her newborn. I went home to splash water on my face and change into clean Levi's and a white cotton blouse.

The day was not as hot as it had been for Shirley's posing, but my forehead was damp from the drive in my blue Chevy pickup. I didn't have air conditioning. I entered the barn wondering what kind of image I would make. I was twenty-six. The muscles of my legs and arms were hard and thick. In high school, I lifted weights until I could heft any sack or box my father could. Today I could carry even heavier ones. I was strong, but not pretty. My face was square, Germanic, bossy-looking. I tried to be particularly nice to those who didn't know me well to make up for this first, daunting impression. But sometimes my face could be my power. People were reluctant to cross me.

"Welcome," Alyson said as I stepped into the shadows behind the studio lights in the barn. She wore a shapeless purple and black batik shift, hemmed mid-calf. Her shoulder length black hair was caught back in a leather clip. She was advancing a roll of film into place in her camera. I was suddenly dumbfounded. There was something alarming about standing in front of a tripod to have your picture taken, like a fashion model or a bride.

I wiped the sweat from my brow. "Hello," I finally said. "I must be one of your last victims."

She nodded, waved at the grey barn wall, and said, "You know what to do, right?" I went to the wall, certain that the camera would capture flaws I myself hadn't noticed—a hair sprouting out of the mole on my cheek, or a chewed fingernail. I felt this sort of self-consciousness before doctor's appointments. I always washed obsessively for them, fighting the odor of my apprehension. I knew I could never be perfectly clean, that even the strongest deodorant soap would leave at least the faint odors of my underarms and genitals behind.

I leaned against the barn wall and waited for her to tell me what to do. What a triumph this must be, I thought, to get the images of so many people on film. They are forever yours, framed and still. I heard a click.

"What are you doing?" I asked, startled, and she snapped the shutter again. "Wait a minute. You're supposed to tell me when," I cried, like a small girl pleading to be warned the moment before the doctor's needle pierces her skin.

"When," Alyson said, deadpan, and kept clicking. "You farm?"

"Yes. Four hundred acres. My father's land and he still helps, but I'm not sure how much longer he can manage," I said.

"You'll inherit it, then?" She scrolled the film forward and clicked again. I was fixated on the ominous sound of it: scroll-click, scroll-click. Unlike a child being vaccinated, I was not easily distracted. I wanted to snap her mouth shut. Her questions were like flies on my skin, irritating me. I didn't want to be there and submit to this reproduction of my bulky hips in their baggy blue jeans, my relentlessly serious face, my skeptical hazel eyes, on film.

"I think I'm the only one interested," I said, and tried to discourage her from talking to me until she was through.

As she rewound the film back through the camera, she asked, "By the way, could you ask Shirley to come back when the baby's out? With the baby?"

"I can ask," I said. I hadn't thought about Shirley since before I'd walked the corn fields. Then it was back, the nervous whisper in my stomach reminding me of the ordeal she was about to go through. I felt like I'd been away from Shirley for a long, far away time, as if I'd flown to France to await the news of the birth of my first niece or nephew. "After all," I said hurriedly, eager to get back near my telephone, "that child will be a resident of Ox Bend too. You wouldn't really have everybody until you get the baby's photo."

We didn't know what to do when my sister's baby came out with only a fourth of his brain. Marshall stumbled into the waiting room to tell me about it, bawling about a half-dead boy. I couldn't get any details from him. Finally the doctor came in to explain that a hole in the neural tube caused it. It happens to two out of every one thousand babies, some making it out as paraplegics, some both paraplegic and mentally handicapped. The ones who get the hole the furthest up have damaged brains and do not live more than a few weeks. That was my sister's son.

Determined to cope, Shirley remained sad but clear-headed. She visited the boy several times a week, gazing from outside the glass incubator at the caved-in section of his head. It looked like something heavy had been thrown at his tiny skull. She and Marshall decided to call the child Clement. "It'll look dignified on the stone," Shirley sighed. She was not pretending anything; it was not in her nature. She hadn't even been good at playing with Barbie dolls when we were children. She got them in the plastic convertibles, drove them around the lawn, and that was about it. They didn't even talk to each other. I designed elaborate scenarios. My doll plays were full of love affairs, accidents, betrayals, bankruptcies, and death.

I was the angry, irrational one. I thought the doctor should have told Shirley she could have had a test early on to find out about the problem. I eyed him so coldly whenever we met in the halls of the hospital that he began to avoid me. As the autumn deepened and harvesting went into full swing, I wore my boots and sweaty jeans right from the fields to the hospital. I wanted him and everyone else in the sterile, cream white halls of the university hospital to see who I was, a woman in charge of harvesting four-hundred rustling acres of corn and beans and prepared to raze their souls just as well.

Clement pressed on into his fourth week. One afternoon as Shirley and I drove to the hospital, she said, "Monona, he's making me so tired."

"Who, Marshall?"

"No, Clement," she said, turning her face to the shorn corn field blanketing the roadside. "I mean, he was in me so heavy and real. I never worried. I never fantasized that something tragic would happen, like some mothers do. Now he's not like other babies, with some crazy schedule of feedings and naps and all that for me to tend to. But at least that way, when he rested, I would have, too. Now I can't rest. He's never at peace. So I can't be either."

I thought of Shirley in the photography studio, challenging Alyson to let her sit down and ease the weight of her pregnant belly. Shirley probably would have gotten herself the chair if Alyson had refused. It wasn't that Shirley was lazy; it just didn't make sense for Shirley to be uncomfortable for the sole purpose of posing for a picture. Shirley would stick out in the array of photographs of Ox Bend residents, as the only one pregnant and the only one sitting down. Everyone would see that picture and shake their heads at the sight of the promise of her belly, a promise everyone now knew had been broken. Then they would look at her face. On that day Shirley's expression had been devoid of any trace of maternal glow. Instead her face was crossed with heat and a peevish annoyance. Maybe they would think she didn't love what was inside her, even the dozens of women who themselves had known this heaviness.

I left Shirley staring at the incubator at the hospital. I drove north through the city to the main campus of the university. I had not seen Alyson Quinn since I'd posed for her. I was certain she knew about what had happened with the baby. A reporter from *The Trumpeter* did an article on it and the town hummed with gossip at every development. People were also talking about Alyson and the photo exhibition, badgering Jack Hussman about when the VFW Lodge would be hosting it. Had she even talked to him about it recently? everyone wondered.

I had not been to the university since my graduation day more than three years ago. I had never been inside the Fine Arts building. It had a curving, dark glass south wall, with long banners advertising upcoming plays hanging in the lobby: "Love Letters," "Landscape of the Body," and an opera, "La Traviata." Alyson Quinn's office was on the third floor. On her door was a poster photograph print of a woman sitting at a desk writing, her back turned. The poster said, "Ad Feminam: Women and Literature. A series from Chrysanthemum Press." Alyson's signature graced the bottom left corner of the print. I read on the chart next to the door that she was in the last quarter hour of her office hours. She also had a class that night, "Introduction to Printmaking." I knocked on the door.

She was surprised to see me. It was as if my presence outside the usual Ox Bend setting was as improbable as the woman on the poster suddenly turning, becoming three-dimensional, and walking away from the desk. "Monona, what can I do for you?" she said, sitting down in her swivel chair. She wore a narrow black skirt and a purple blazer. Hammered brass earrings in the shape of narrow crescents hung in her ears. She gestured to a swivel chair beside hers, but I remained standing.

"I was wondering if you could give me those pictures of my sister," I said nervously. I rubbed my tongue over the rough tops of my upper molars.

"My God. Oh. I heard what happened. I am very sorry," Alyson said.

"Yes, I am too," I said. "It hasn't been easy on us." She asked how the baby was doing. "Well, I don't think he'll be with us much longer." I asked her again for the photographs of Shirley.

"You want copies?" Alyson said. "That won't be a problem. Just give me a couple of days to develop the negatives."

"Actually, Alyson, I want the negatives. Any prints you've made. Everything."

"I'm not sure I understand."

"I don't think they should be in the exhibition. I think that's our right, to say where we should and shouldn't be pinned up on a wall."

"This is what Shirley thinks?" Alyson asked.

"Yes," I said. Though I really had no idea what Shirley thought at this point, I was sure it would eventually pain her to have the photos exhibited in town.

"I'm sorry," Alyson said. "But unfortunately I'm not in a position to give the photos back to anyone now. I've negotiated a book contract for the Ox Bend Project. The publishers especially like the photos of Shirley."

"A book contract?"

"It's going to be really nice for the town. It'll put it on the map. I'll open the exhibition when the book comes out and it'll be a real draw for outsiders, probably even for people outside of Iowa."

"I don't want my sister's picture in the show, or in a book," I said.

"I'd be willing to explain things to Shirley," Alyson said.

"The hospital visits have been keeping her busy."

"I don't know what to tell you, then. It sounds like this situation would concern her more than it would you," Alyson said, glancing at the clock above her desk. "I have to go now."

"I'll be seeing you, then," I said and walked out.

I found Shirley in the hospital cafeteria, getting a refill of black coffee. She never had coffee without anything in it. "All they have is this powdered cream garbage," she explained. Her eyes were half-closed and her face was puffed with fatigue.

"Why are you drinking that? If you're having trouble relaxing, drinking that at five in the evening isn't going to help you," I said. I looked at the line-up of plastic-wrapped tuna fish and ham sandwiches, of blueberry yogurt, apples, and danishes sticky with yellow custard and sugar glaze. I had a headache from hunger and anger, but I couldn't imagine putting anything to my lips.

"And as if it was that easy, Monona," Shirley said, sitting down at a table. She sat on the edge of the orange plastic chair, her shoulders hunched up, as if she were ready to bolt out of her seat at any moment.

"I just think you probably need all the help you can get and drinking that isn't going to help. You know you were supposed to cut down on caffeine with the baby." I was thinking of my pregnant English teacher at the university. While walking us through the "American Literary Tradition," she drank a strange potion of coffee diluted with hot water. "It's about a six-to-one proportion," she explained, laughing that she'd just needed a taste of coffee to sustain her. Her name was Ms. Gulliani. We watched her belly expand that semester. She had a healthy baby boy during finals week. He would be in kindergarden by now.

Shirley was staring at me. Then I began the slow sinking as I realized what I'd said. I would drown in my regret, I thought.

"Coffee's not goddamned vodka. You just don't get it, do you? I don't need you to tell me this. Millions of women didn't get what I got, after drinking worse than coffee, smoking their lungs out more than I ever have, shooting up, starving themselves, breaking every rule in the book."

I closed my eyes, lids trembling. This was not what I had wanted out of myself.

"And another thing," she continued. "Get the chip off your shoulder. You look like a freak, walking around the hospital giving everyone dirty looks. I'm embarrassed to see you walk in like some psychotic avenging her sister's problem. Did I ask for this act? I don't think so."

"No, you didn't."

"I don't need to look at your sorry face right now, Monona. But let me tell you, all this is going to pass. Because things screw up. The doctor did a little. Nature did a lot. When you can't fix things, the best thing is to keep on trying not to screw things up more."

I got up to leave. "Are you going to need a ride home?" I asked.

"No, Marshall can pick me up."

I wove through the tables and chairs toward the exit of the cafeteria. The room was beginning to fill up for dinner. No one seemed to know what to do, though. Women clutching their large purses and men with their hands in their pockets hovered around the food lines, uncertain about whether to head for the entree line, the sandwich line, or the snack line. The people must be new visitors, unfamiliar with the workings of the cafeteria and the brightly-lit corridors. They were used to everyone eating and sleeping at home, to everyone being well. I was rude to them. I rushed out, elbowing my way to the door. I knew exactly where I wanted to be—outside, on the road, weaving my truck through fields where the harvest was proceeding as it always had, strips of bare, brown earth gradually revealed in the wake of the combines.

In Ox Bend, a town of aging buildings and trust, break-ins were rare but they were not difficult. At Alyson's studio, I pried open a side window with a crowbar. In a small back office room, I found her desk. I went through shadowy stacks of paper, feeling through the soft, torn edges of envelopes, narrow strips of store receipts, the linen texture of stationery. I anticipated the dry crinkle of the onion paper envelopes used for negatives, the smooth humid feel of a photo print. Some piles were of notebooks and hard-covered, glossy-paged volumes, probably art textbooks. The piles yielded nothing. I could find no trace of the fact that 210 people had paraded through this barn to stand before her lens.

I grew bolder and switched on my flashlight, sweeping the narrow glow across the main room of the studio. In contrast to her cluttered office, this room was sparse. Nothing hung on the walls. There were only a few collapsed tripods, four of her powerful lamps, and a half dozen of the folding chairs stacked in a pile next to one wall. Several leather camera bags, dark and wrinkled like sleeping reptiles, were stored on a set of those do-it-yourself metal shelves I'd seen on display in the hardware store. She must keep her work somewhere else, I thought. Perhaps at the university. Despondent, I considered stealing one of her cameras, then decided I wanted nothing of them. I'd never used anything more complicated than a Polaroid. I scanned the flashlight beam from corner to corner, caught a glimpse of table legs, and moved closer.

On the wooden table top, a chamois cloth covered something with a flat, rectangular shape. Underneath the soft, grey cloth was a framed photograph, about three feet long and a foot-and-a-half high. I expected a portrait, a sample of the Ox Bend project, a housewife's eyes peering out at me, shadowed by black mascara-coated eyelashes, or perhaps a beef farmer's pot belly and serious, weathered face. Instead I saw the long black-topped stretch of Second Street West, a cloudless expanse of sky, and the figures of myself and Shirley at the far end of the road. Our backs were to the camera. Though on that day we had been approaching the south turn onto Central that leads to the Ideal Cafe, the photo caught nothing of downtown. We looked small and isolated, the empty road and the endless curly rows of soybeans blanketing out beside us. My back was tensed in an insistent, worried square as I held Shirley's elbow. Even from behind, you could tell she was pregnant. Her shoulders were thrown back and her legs were slightly bowed.

The photograph was in a mahogany frame and covered with a pane of non-glare glass. A large shipping box lay next to the table. Full of styrofoam peanuts, the box was addressed to The Williams Gallery, 113 East Fourth Street, Cincinnati, Ohio. I picked up the framed photograph, set it upright on the table, and leaned it against the wall.

It was beautiful. Shirley and I looked poetic, a pair of sisters walking forever. The soybeans would always be a month before harvest, the sky would always be relentlessly clear, Shirley would always be pregnant, her body tired but rich with promise. But the picture, framed and ready for display, angered me. This was nothing either of us had given Alyson permission to do. Yes, the town had agreed to pose. We had all stood before her, we had all been patient and cooperative. But Alyson had gone ahead and taken more. Had she shot photos of others, too, lurking around Ox Bend like a sniper? Or were Shirley and I her only prey, her special fascination? I was suddenly dizzy with fury, as if I myself were to be slipped into that box, smothered with the styrofoam peanuts, on my way with my grieving—and now estranged—sister to be stared at by people we would never know.

When I threw the flashlight down, I did not quite believe I was capable of breaking anything. I expected the glass to resist the blow, as the type of plastic used for children's glasses do. But the glass shattered and the flashlight bulb cracked. In the darkness, I made my way out of the barn, my hands touching the metal backs of folding chairs, the bundled legs of the tripods, those cold, smooth objects like the bare bones of skeletons guiding my way.

Forty Acres

Rose Hamilton-Gottlieb

"Why don't you and Jens just pack up the kids and come on out here to California?" The sentence, read for the fourth time, still shocked Louella. She put down the letter and took a deep breath. The window rattled in a gust of wind and she shivered, although it was warm enough in the kitchen. Three-year-old Amy climbed up on a chair beside her and reached for the tablet. Louella tore off a sheet for her to scribble on.

"Think about it, anyway," her sister had written. Louella Hartin had done little else since she'd taken Julie's letter from the mailbox the day before. This morning she'd waited until the three older kids had left for the school bus and Jens had gone outside before opening it again. "Most of the time the sun shines and it's warm," Julie's letter went on,

> *and the ocean is like nothing you ever imagined. I know you've seen pictures, but pictures don't show how it sounds or what it feels like to wade in the surf or the smell that blows in over water that goes on forever. The only thing close I can think of is when we were kids and we ran barefoot over the fields just after the plow had gone through. Remember how it felt cold and smooth when we put our feet down and then it would crumble under our weight? And the spring smell that came up from it? The next day it would be hard and rough, so we only did that once a year. Well, out here we have the beach all year round. Flowers too, even in the dead of winter, only there's no such thing as dead of winter here. That's when everything's green. You wouldn't believe the trees that bloom. I don't mean fruit trees; I mean trees that flower just for the fun of it. Purple Jacarandas and red flame trees and white magnolias.*

"Mama, there's a man out there," Amy said. Louella put down the letter and went to the window. She watched the visitor climb out of a brand new car. A green 1946 Packard. He gazed at the brown fields and pasture, a patchwork stitched with barbed wire and a dirt road that rose and fell over the hills. A hunter, by the looks of the red cap. She hated pheasant season when men from the city swarmed over the fields, so anxious to make a kill they had to wear bright colors to keep from bagging each other. That was another thing Julie didn't have to worry about anymore. There were no guns on the streets of Los Angeles.

The man squared his shoulders as if inhaling deeply, then walked over to shake hands with Jens, who was hitching Charlie and Bess to the wagon. She recognized him then. It was Lucas Reardon, whose aunt and uncle had owned and lived on the Hartin Place when he was a child. His aunt still owned the east forty, but rented it out to a local farmer. Lucas came out from Des Moines every fall to hunt along the fencerows. He always came to the house to ask permission to hunt along the creek in their east pasture.

Louella went back to Julie's letter. "Ted is working a lot of overtime at the factory, but when he leaves his job, he doesn't have to think about it until he goes back the next day. The pay is good, too; in fact, we're saving for a new car. We go to the movies almost every week, and I've made up my mind that this year we're going to the Rose Parade." Louella had seen pictures of the Rose Parade in *Life* magazine and had marveled that on the first day of January when Iowa was likely to be freezing cold, there could be a day anywhere so full of flowers and sunshine. Until now, it hadn't occurred to her that she might see it for herself.

"The kids didn't have hardly any colds last winter, not like when we were in Iowa. Remember the winter before last when George had bronchitis for months on end?" Louella glanced at Amy, who was dressed for the field in a flannel shirt and snowpants. Last year, she coughed from January through March.

"You and me could help each other out with the kids. It's not right that cousins should grow up not knowing each other. Remember how we used to go to Aunt Jennie's and play with Harold and Ruby?" Louella remembered. They had visited their cousins weekly, and Aunt Jennie was always there to help her mother feed thrashers or can tomatoes.

"I know Ted could get Jens on at the factory." Louella put down the letter and frowned. That was the part she couldn't imagine, Jens working in a factory.

"Mama, they're coming in the house," Amy said from the window. Louella looked down at her overalls. She didn't like to be seen dressed for the field, but she wasn't going to run and change clothes for Lucas Reardon. She fed a handful of dry corncobs to the fire in the cookstove and filled the coffee pot from the water bucket. Then she sat down, covering Julie's letter with her tablet.

Jens and Lucas wiped their feet on the back porch and came in. "Morning, Mrs. Hartin," Lucas said, cap in hand. He looked longingly around the kitchen, at the ice box, the cast iron cookstove, the washstand with its water bucket and dipper. "Lots of memories here." Nostalgic, as usual, about things that made their life hard. Jens pulled a chair out for Lucas and the men sat down. "I won't keep you long. I remember what corn picking season was like. I hear folks out this way got good crops this year."

Jens nodded. "We should get at least fifty bushels to the acre."

If the weather holds long enough to get it out of the fields, thought Louella.

Lucas shook his head. "I'm afraid Aunt Marge's forty acres won't yield that much."

"That land's wore out," said Jens.

"Well, it sure don't bring in much income."

"You can't plant corn one year after another and get a decent yield."

"I always wondered why that piece wasn't sold with the rest of the farm," Louella said.

"It probably should have been, but it nearly killed Aunt Marge when my uncle died and she had to sell out. She kept that piece, thinking to build on it some day and move back. When that didn't work out, she thought her son might want it. What it finally boiled down to was, she couldn't stand to let it go. Can't say I blame her; I'm kind of attached to this place myself."

"Maybe you'd like to buy our eighty acres and take up farming," Louella said. She met Jens's surprised stare with a steady look. When she heard the coffee pot threaten to boil over, she got up and moved the pot to the back of the stove.

Lucas laughed. "Well now, I might be tempted, Mrs. Hartin, if I could afford it with my boy in college and my daughters' weddings to pay for, and if I didn't think I was too old to learn how to farm with these new machines. Ask me again in ten years when I'm ready to retire from the grocery business. Maybe I'd make a good gentleman farmer." He laughed again. "No, what I came out here for, besides getting in some hunting, was to sell Jens here Aunt Marge's forty acres."

"She's selling, is she?" Jens said, taking a pack of cigarettes from the pocket of his overalls and offering one to Lucas. Amy, who had crawled onto his lap, pursed her lips, ready to blow out the match.

"Well, not exactly," Lucas said. "She passed away two months ago and the family decided to sell. We all agreed that she would have liked to see that land returned to the original farm. That's why I wanted to talk to you first, before we put it on the market."

Louella set cups of coffee in front of the men and moved the cream pitcher closer to Lucas.

"It's in pretty bad shape," Jens said. He poured cream in his coffee and let Amy stir, keeping his hold on the handle of the cup. He was interested, Louella could tell. He was probably thinking that the hogs had brought a good price and the corn was turning out to be a bumper crop—not a bad time to buy more land.

"That's the trouble with renting out farmland," Lucas said. "Renters don't always think about whether it will be any good for the next generation. That's one reason we'd like to see you have it. Anyway, given the state it's in, we'll let it go to you for thirty-three-dollars an acre."

Louella almost spilled her coffee. They had paid one-hundred-and-twenty-dollars an acre for the rest of the farm; they'd be fools to pass up this deal. Then she remembered Julie's letter, hidden on the table between them. If he buys this land, she thought, it will be that much harder to leave.

Jens gently removed the spoon from Amy's fingers and lifted the cup to his mouth, smearing his moustache with cream. "Tell you what," he said. "Let me see how the crop comes in, see if I have any corn to sell." What he really meant, Louella knew, was that he had to see if the Land Bank would re-do the mortgage.

"Fair enough. Just don't keep us waiting too long."

Louella glanced from one man to the other. Lucas looked soft, with nervous ways, like a man who works hard at something he doesn't especially like and maybe drinks a little too much. But he was talking about retiring in ten years and coming back to the land as a gentleman farmer, and he had a son in college and money enough to give his daughters big weddings.

Compared to Lucas, Jens was solid and strong from working

outdoors all his life, but it was hard work even for a younger man. Above the tan line on his forehead, his scalp showed a fragile white through his thin grey hair. He was fifty-three and getting tired. As she watched, he helped Amy to a sip of his coffee, and she realized that a stranger would take her for his granddaughter. His youngest child was only three, and if he had his way about having another boy, she wouldn't be the last. Jens would have to work until he dropped into his grave.

Louella felt a sudden surge of anger toward Lucas Reardon, offering his ruined land. Jens would bring it back, of course. He would burn off the stubble of this year's crop and plow the potash into the soil and cover it with a good layer of manure before planting it to corn. But he would have to shovel every inch of that manure from the feedlot into the horse-drawn manure spreader. It would take him a month just to prepare the field. Jens knew how to farm and he would restore the land, but who would restore Jens?

"Tell you what," Lucas said, draining his cup. "Joe Marshall over in Ralston is handling the sale. I'll tell him not to advertise it until he hears from you." He rose from the table, gave a little tug to one of Amy's braids, and zipped his jacket. "Nice pair of bays out there."

"Good workers, too. I can cultivate an acre of corn an hour with them." Jens lifted Amy onto the floor and got up from the table and grabbed his cap.

Lucas nodded at Louella. "Not too many still using horses," he said as he followed Jens out the door. She watched them through the window. Jens adjusted the harness and Lucas ran his hands over Charlie's withers and offered something from his pocket to Bess, reminiscing, no doubt, about his own childhood spent in the fields behind a team. She went back to the table and did some quick calculations on her tablet. The price of the land was only thirteen-hundred-and-twenty-dollars, but that would be added onto the original loan of almost ten-thousand, plus four percent interest and more taxes. She watched the Packard climb the hill to the east and park alongside the road. Jens had finished hitching up the horses, so she put away her letter writing things and helped Amy into her coat and tied a wool scarf under her chin.

"This is red, isn't it?" Amy asked, fingering the scarf.

"That's right," Louella said, and added to herself, so the stupid hunters from the city won't take you for a pheasant.

They picked side by side. Jens stayed in the outer row because he was always ahead of her and had more control of where he threw the corn. Louella grabbed the tip of an ear of corn with her right hand and raked the shucking hook strapped to her left hand across the bottom of the ear, then snapped it off, leaving the shuck on the dry cornstalk. Then she tossed the ear against the bang board that jutted up on the opposite side of the wagon and it dropped down into the wagon bed, which was already half-full. She was careful not to hit Amy, asleep in the corner, on top of the corn.

"What did you think you were doing back there, asking Lucas if he wanted to buy the farm?" Jens asked.

She had wondered how long it would take him to get around to that. He'd hardly said a word since they left the house, probably waiting for her to bring up Lucas's offer. But she could wait him out any day. She tried to keep it light. "Well, he was so taken with the house, and he always looks like a lovesick dog when he gets out of his car and looks over the fields, I thought he might just make us an offer."

Jens grunted. She wondered if he was annoyed because she had offered up the farm or if he thought she had spoken out of turn. Probably both. Well, maybe she ought to speak out of turn once in awhile.

They reached the end of the field and, without being told, the horses turned around. The wagon creaked and groaned on its axles, and in a rush of wings and harsh croaks, a pheasant flew up from the cover of brush along the fencerow. It circled overhead and landed on a post, balancing its plump body with its long, sweeping tail. Its rusty brown feathers blended in with the dried cornstalks and the weathered wood of the fence post, but the iridescent blue and scarlet of its head, ringed with the white on its throat, made it a prime target.

"Would you look at that," Jens said, "Perched right out in the open like he never heard of hunting season. And me without the shotgun."

"He's too pretty to kill," Louella said, glad that Jens didn't really like to hunt.

Jens handed her an ear of corn, "The best one yet." She took it and turned it over in her palm. It was heavy, filled out clear to the tip with rock hard kernels that had rough, almost sharp edges. She nodded, handing it back. He dropped it into a gunny sack tied to the inside of the wagon bed. The bag was almost full.

It usually took a whole season of picking to fill the five or six bags with prize corn to be saved back for seed, but this year there were already five bags put away.

Louella felt divided. It was wonderful to see all Jens's hard work pay off. On the other hand, the idea of going to California, far-fetched though it was, had taken root. This clearly was not the year to persuade him to give up farming.

They worked in silence for awhile, Jens moving over into Louella's row when she fell behind. There was a rhythm to their movements, in the swish of the shucking hook, the almost simultaneous crack of the ear as it snapped off, followed by its crash against the bang board. And over it all, the wind dipped through the dried grass and rustled the cornstalks.

Louella's feet and hands were cold, and she was tired. At least Amy was getting a nap. She'd been good, spending the first hour trudging behind the wagon, picking up fallen ears and putting them in a pile. Then, when they came to a low place along the fencerow where rainwater drained off, she had played in the little pocket of sand while they made a couple of turns in the field.

When they reached the front of the wagon, the team pulled ahead and the wagon creaked over the half-frozen ground, snapping cornstalks as it went. The horses stopped when the pickers were exactly one wagon length behind, then stretched their necks to bite off fresh ears of corn.

"What do you think about Lucas's offer?" asked Jens.

"Well, I don't know," she said, and she didn't know. The farmer in her wanted to say, yes, of course. We can't pass it up. The part that longed to see a body of water larger than a farm pond was saying no, we're in deep enough as it is. Let's get out while we can.

"We'll never get it cheaper," he said.

"You said yourself it was in bad shape."

"Nothing a good layer of manure won't cure."

"Seems to me you got about all you can handle right now."

"If we buy that land, we can put in another field of oats and still have forty acres of corn."

"We've never had more than thirty and sometimes it takes us a month to pick that."

"Will's in first grade. Won't be long until he'll be out here." He sent her a sly look without breaking the rhythm. "All the more reason to have that other boy."

That other boy. Jens talked as if his second son already existed somewhere and all she had to do was open a door and he'd appear. She wondered how many more daughters she'd bear before she found that other boy behind the door.

They kept going as they talked, nothing breaking the tear-crack-crash-thud, Louella two beats behind so it was like a round. The corn piled up in the wagon, making a fortress around the child asleep in the corner. The sun came out and it was as if the pot at the end of every Iowa rainbow had been tipped up and emptied into their wagon bed. They both paused at the same time, causing Charlie's ears to pick up. "That's farmer's gold," Jens said.

Louella nodded, thinking, or fool's gold.

They picked on, until Louella, her hand raised to throw an ear of corn, was startled by the sound of a shotgun close by. Charlie and Bess stamped their feet and snorted, and without thinking, Louella stepped forward just as Jens threw an ear of corn. It struck her on the temple and forced her glasses against her nose, bringing tears to her eyes. There was another blast, and Jens grabbed the horses' reigns to keep them from bolting. "You all right?" he yelled over his shoulder. Dazed, Louella looked at the ear of corn in her hand, threw it to the ground, and stomped off, shouting behind her as she went. "That's it. We're moving to California."

Louella stumbled through the field, tripping over broken-down cornstalks. She was halfway to the house when she remembered Amy asleep in the wagon. As she started back for her, the noon whistle from Casey sounded from a mile- and-a-half to the east and she stopped in her tracks. She heard the muted whistle from Adair, six miles to the west. Then, very faintly, and only because the wind was in the right direction, the call came from Guthrie Center, ten miles to the North. All of Guthrie County would stop work for the noon meal. She hesitated. Jens would be coming in to unload and eat dinner anyway. Besides, she needed time to think about those surprising words that had come, unbidden, from her lips.

Louella was glad she'd left Amy in the field when she opened the screen door to the back porch and saw two pheasants on a blood-soaked newspaper. Lucas, who always shared his kill with them. She loaded them into a pan, trying not to see the scarlet plumage of the male, darkened with blood, and carried them down into the cave. Later, she'd clean them for supper.

They ate pork chops and potatoes in silence, listening to the market report on the radio. The price of corn was up to eighty cents a bushel, mostly due to a July hailstorm that had struck most of the northeastern part of the state, for once leaving their farm untouched.

After Amy finished eating and wandered off into the front room, Jens pushed his chair back from the table and lit his pipe. "Now what was that business about California?" he asked. She handed him Julie's letter and got up to stack the dishes. When he had finished reading, he put it aside. "My God woman, are you crazy?"

"Probably," she said. She stood at the work table, her back to him, washing the plates. "Sometimes I think we're both crazy to try to make a living this way."

"And what the hell would we do in California?"

"Julie said you could get on at the factory." She rinsed the last plate and stacked it upright in the drainer.

"The factory? You want me to be a slave in a factory?"

She turned to face him. He wasn't angry, which surprised her. It was more like he was curious to explore just how crazy she was before carting her off to the state mental hospital at Clarinda. She wasn't sure herself she wasn't losing her mind, but she'd started something, so she pressed on.

"I suppose you're not working like a slave now?"

That did it. He pounded the table with his fist, tipping over the cream pitcher. "I ain't no slave. I'm a farmer. I own this land and that makes me my own boss. I work when I feel like it and I put my feet up and read the paper when I feel like it. I decide what to plant and when to plant it and how much seed to put in the ground. Ain't nobody making me punch no damn time clock."

Louella turned back to the dishes. It was no use arguing that the market determined everything he did, that the fact that he decided whether he got up at 5:00 a.m. or 6:00 a.m. didn't make him free because the cows couldn't wait much later to be milked. No use reminding him that right now he had no choice but to get back into the corn field before the weather changed. So she kept her back turned and her mouth shut.

In bed beside Jens, Louella drifted off, her mind and muscles still tuned into the tear-crack-crash-thud rhythm of the corn field, when his voice intruded. "What the hell did you think you were talking about anyway, saying we ought to go gallivanting off to California?"

She beat her way up through the fog of near sleep. So he'd been nursing a grudge against her for wanting something that he wouldn't—or couldn't—give her. "Do we have to talk about this now?"

He ignored the question. Jens had trouble sleeping when something was on his mind. And why should I sleep when he can't? she thought.

"You know I can't just pick up and leave. Who'd take care of the livestock?"

Somebody, she thought wearily. Anybody. Sell them. But let me get some rest. Out loud, she said, "I don't say we should go. I just say think about it. Maybe life doesn't have to be this hard."

"Well, if it's too hard for you, maybe I should buy you a bus ticket to California."

"You just do that," she said, awake enough now to be mad. "And while you're at it, get tickets for the kids. I'll go to work in that factory myself. Now let me get some sleep."

He was quiet for awhile. Then, just as she dared hope the subject was closed, he said, "Well, you do what you want. Tomorrow I'm going to Winston to see the land agent."

She didn't answer, and after awhile Jens started to snore gently. Louella poked him in the shoulder to make him turn over, but it didn't matter now if he snored or not. She was wide awake and too tired to sleep. She lay in bed for awhile and listened to the restless leaves scuttling along the sidewalk and piling up against the side of the house. When she heard the whistle from the 11:15 westbound train, she got up and pulled a wool sweater over her flannel nightgown. In the kitchen, she lit a kerosene lamp and dropped a handful of coal onto the dying embers of the cookstove. She moved the lamp to the edge of the table and pulled a chair as close to the open oven as she could and still have enough light to read by.

She scanned the first part of Julie's letter, but this time, with the kerosene lamp throwing her shadow up against the stove pipe, there was no sense of excitement. It was as if the middle-of-the-night darkness, which pressed in from outside and muffled everything but the steady beat of the clock, muffled dreams as well. How could she have even considered the idea? She might imagine herself going to a place that had different rhythms, but Jens was tied to this place. The Hartin Place, as he liked to call it. And she was tied to him. It wasn't likely she would ever see the ocean or the mountains. She would have to content herself with the view from the top of Jens's hill.

She turned to the last paragraph of Julie's letter.

We took a drive up to the mountains last Sunday, hoping to see some fall color, but it's been too warm for Jack Frost. The sycamore in our yard is turning, but so far the leaves are only a yellowish brown. When the sun hits it right, I pretend it's fall, but its really a poor counterfeit. Did you see many pheasants this year? Ted went dove hunting last week with some men from the factory. He didn't bring any home for me to cook, and I was glad. Can you imagine killing a dove? I hear them early in the morning and they make a soft, lonesome sound.

Louella pulled her chair up to the table and filled her fountain pen with ink and began. "Dear Julie, California sounds awfully nice, but we won't be coming out there any time soon. Jens has a chance to buy the forty acres just east of here real cheap." She went on to describe the new coat she had made for Mary and how tall Jane was getting, and how Willie was learning to milk the cows. And she said she was sending along Amy's "letter" which contained all the words she had learned while playing school with Mary. She poured her life onto the pages, drowning out any other life she might imagine for herself, adding, at the end, "When you get your new car, maybe you can load up the kids and come home for a visit."

Before folding the pages, Louella glanced over Julie's letter one last time. Her eyes rested for a moment on the last two lines: "Promise me you'll think about the possibility of moving out here. It's scary at first, but you'd be surprised how many people you meet from back home."

"Think about the possibility," Julie had written. Louella lay down the pen and took a jagged breath. That was what she couldn't accept, that there were no other possibilities for her to think about. It wasn't that she wanted to leave the farm so much as she wanted to be able to entertain the idea of leaving. She wanted to be able to talk about possibilities. Jens had his dreams; why couldn't she have a dream that was separate from his, a possibility that didn't originate with Jens Hartin? One that she didn't have to keep to herself to keep the peace?

Louella sat for a long time, while the lumps of burned-out coal dropped, one by one, through the grate into the ash drawer. Then she got up and went to the windowsill for the iridescent blue feather she had plucked from the pheasant's neck. She tiptoed over the linoleum in the front room and took a perfect red maple leaf from her mother's bible. She tucked these in with her letter to California.

The Flood Summer

Patricia Stevens

At Mel's Grocery, Delia stood in front of a neighborhood bulletin board covered with messages about everything from lost cats and dogs, to lawn-mowing and babysitting services, to tarot-card and psychic readings. In the far lower lefthand corner she made space by moving a three-by-five notecard, someone selling a rowing machine, a little to the right. Delia, however, wasn't selling anything. She had no service to offer and she hadn't lost a pet, either. What Delia had lost was a daughter.

At the top of the board she located two free push pins and secured her flyer to the cork, one pin at the top of the paper, one at the bottom. *MISSING*, it began. *Please help me find my daughter Stacey Lynne. She is 17 years old, 5'5", 122 pounds, hazel eyes, and shoulder length light brown hair, sometimes blond. Last seen June 28, at the corner of Lincoln and 10th, wearing cut-off Levi's and a black leather vest.* The flyer included a photograph of Stacey at sixteen, wearing an angora sweater and holding Snowball, the long-haired white cat she'd picked out at the pound on her seventh birthday. Delia was somewhat disappointed in the picture—it was a bit fuzzy and the Kodacolor didn't translate very well into black and white—and she worried that Stacey wouldn't be recognized.

Delia took a moment to stare at her baby, the baby she gave birth to, searching Stacey's eyes for an answer. The first time Stacey ran off, Delia had a hard time believing that her daughter could leave Snowball behind. But this time there was an even larger question: Stacey had not only abandoned Snowball, she had also left behind her eight-month-old daughter Hadley.

Now under Delia's care, Hadley was in her stroller, sucking on a pacifier while keeping an eye on Delia as she pinned the flyers in all the grocery stores and on all the bulletin boards in town. Delia had a hundred flyers and had already tacked up at least twenty-five. She could have done a lot more in this same amount of time, but it was raining, as it had done all of June and now into July. For weeks Delia had rivulets of water meandering along her basement floor. Her entire house felt heavy with humidity, and she was tired of wiping the moisture off the sills where the rain came in at a slant through the open windows.

Leaving her car parked in front of Mel's, Delia put the flyers back into the plastic bag she'd been carrying them in and slid them into the pocket at the back of Hadley's stroller. She shot open the huge striped beach umbrella that easily protected both her and Hadley and headed down the street toward the community center where there were cork boards in two different locations.

It was after 2:30 by the time Delia started for home, and fifty-eight of the Stacey flyers remained. She had wanted to nail some on telephone poles at strategic locations, but the rain would have turned them to pulp and Hadley was tired and cranky and Delia wanted to get her home and into her own bed. On the way, though, Hadley fell asleep in her car seat in the back of Delia's tan Ford Tempo. Although Delia tried very hard to keep Hadley awake—she played the radio too loudly, whistled along to the music, shouted out Hadley's name every minute or two—her attempts were in vain.

Delia pulled the car into the garage, got out, checked on Hadley who was slumped in her car seat, then went into the kitchen, leaving the door open behind her so she could hear Hadley if she woke up. From experience she knew that if she took Hadley out of the car and tried to put her into her crib, the little girl would wake up and be irritable for the rest of the day. This way Delia could work in the kitchen while Hadley took her nap in the car.

As Delia washed her hands in the kitchen sink, Snowball bounded in from the bedrooms and circled around her feet. For an eleven-year-old, Snowball still had a lot of pep, even though he missed Stacey terribly, maybe even more than Hadley did, Delia sometimes thought. Every day Snowball tried at least once to enter Stacey's room. Delia knew he just wanted to curl up and sleep against the pillows on Stacey's bed, but she kept the door closed anyway. Hadley's crib was in the same room, and Delia once heard a story about a cat that curled up on top of a baby's head and smothered him.

After Delia dumped dry catfood into Snowball's empty bowl, she took a package of chicken out of the refrigerator. It was still not completely thawed, so she unwrapped it and sprinkled a little salt over the skin. As she did this, she noticed that the red light on her answering machine was blinking. Pushing the chicken aside, she moved toward the phone. Before Stacey left, Delia loved seeing the blinking light, but now she was afraid of it—the evil red eye. Lately, whenever Delia rewound her answering machine, her heart pounded in panic as she imagined the sound of the voice that just might report the death of her daughter. Would it be the deep male sound of a state cop? The youthful voice of an emergency-room doctor at some faraway hospital? The slurred speech of a drug-addicted boyfriend? At least three or four times each day she spent several minutes in stark terror wondering if Stacey were dead or alive. Wondering if she would succumb to drugs, prostitution, a boyfriend who beat her up. But as soon as the tape began to play and she heard Andy's voice, Delia let out a sigh of relief. "It's me," he said. "I'm running a little late and probably won't get off until 5:30. By the time I get to your place, 6:00. This rain. What a bitch, huh? All the underground lines are wet. Thousands of repair calls again today." Delia's own phone lines were scratchy all the time now, too, but Andy said there was little that could be done until the rain stopped. But there was more rain in the forecast. Record-setting rain. Several rivers in the state had already spilled over their banks.

Delia took out a plastic bag, dumped flour, salt, pepper, thyme, and paprika into it, then put the pieces of chicken in and started shaking them around. After heating the oil in her electric skillet, she dropped in the legs, thighs, breasts, and wings, one at a time. The skin on the chicken sizzled and the oil spat out at her, but Delia was smiling. She was thinking about how lucky she was to have found Andy, who was far and away the most considerate, the most gentle man she had ever been with. At first she was apprehensive about their age difference: she was a few weeks short of forty, he was only thirty-four. But she was over that now, and last week when she was combing his chest hair with her fingers, she was delighted to find a gray one. Delia now believed that had she not known Andy, she might be in the psych ward this very minute, that's how upset she was over Stacey's disappearance. But Andy was right there for her, even though he and Stacey didn't much get along. He was never mean to her—in Delia's mind, he was not even rude. Stacey just resented his very presence, just as she resented the presence of any man Delia had ever been with—other than Stacey's father, of course, a man who disappeared from both Stacey's and Delia's life more than twelve years ago and only resurfaced twice, both times for not more than two or three hours.

When Delia met Andy life seemed to take a 180-degree turn for the better. Life was so good Delia even believed that Stacey would get off the drugs forever.

As Delia turned the chicken with a pair of metal tongs, she heard Hadley babbling to herself in the car. "Grandma's right here, Hadley," she shouted out toward the garage. She never wanted Hadley to have the slightest fear of abandonment.

Hadley stopped cooing to listen.

"That's right, Baby. Grandma Dee is right here in the kitchen coming to get you in one short minute."

By the time Delia had turned all the chicken, Hadley was whimpering in the back of the Ford. Hurriedly, she rinsed her hands, wiped them on a faded dish towel, and ran into the garage, which was only ten feet away. She didn't like to hear Hadley cry. Now that she was a grandmother, she saw no reason that a baby should have to cry for more than a minute or two. She and Stacey had had several terrible arguments over this very issue.

Delia lifted Hadley out of the car and patted her on the back. "Don't cry, Baby," she said. "Grandma Dee-Dee would never, ever, ever leave her precious Hadley." Hadley responded by staring into Delia's face and pulling on one of her earrings, the long, dangly, beaded kind, which were simply too irresistible for a baby not to grab. As she stood near the open garage door, Delia tried to distract her. "Look, Hadley. At the rain." It had been raining since the previous night, a moderate but steady rain. It was almost as if it had never not been raining. All the wood inside Delia's house was swollen so that the windows and doors were hard to open and close. "The year without a summer," some people were calling it. Front-page cartoons in *The Des Moines Register* showed the governor directing animals and people onto an ark. Because it happened five times a week, the rain held no fascination for

Hadley. But Delia stared and stared out into it thinking of Stacey, wondering if she were still in the city, still in the Midwest even, if she had shelter from the deluge (she left this time with only the clothes on her back), or if she had gone south again, to Texas, or west to Los Angeles.

When Hadley began to pull a strand of Delia's hair, Delia shifted the baby to her hip and carried her into the kitchen. She noticed that some of the younger mothers wore their babies on their backs, or if they were infants, in pouches on their fronts, but Delia let Hadley ride on her left hip where she seemed to feel the most secure. After Stacey vanished, Hadley cried uncontrollably for three days, and there was little Delia could do to comfort her. It was eerie, really, the way Hadley knew that something had changed, even though Stacey was often gone for entire weekends, leaving Delia in charge. Delia's sister Ginny, who lived in Marshalltown and had four grandchildren, told Delia over the phone that babies were born with a sixth sense, but as they got older, unless they used it, they would lose it. "Horse pucky," Delia said when she heard it, but she let Hadley travel on her hip from that moment on.

And this arrangement did not seem to slow Delia down one bit. She could still vacuum, dust furniture, load the dishwasher, take out the garbage, even sweep the kitchen floor. The other night Andy was sitting at the dinner table watching her clear the dishes while Hadley bounced along on her hip. "Aren't you afraid of spoiling her?" he asked. It was the first time he'd judged anything about the way Delia was taking care of Hadley.

"It won't be long and I'll be back to work, then she'll be in daycare and she'll be lucky if she gets picked up," Delia snapped. Since Stacey's disappearance, Delia had been on vacation from her job at Allied Insurance where she worked in the billing department.

"That's what I mean," Andy said.

But Delia dropped it. Andy had nieces and nephews but no kids of his own. How could he be expected to understand? Besides, no one knew what Hadley needed better than Delia—least of all Stacey, who simply had not seen the value of Delia's experience as a mother.

Andy appeared at 6:00, just as he said he would. That was one of the things Delia appreciated about him—his reliability. Delia figured that if she added up the time she spent just waiting for men to arrive, it would turn into years. Andy was at the kitchen door off the garage, carrying a cardboard palette loaded with six plastic bottled-water jugs. With Hadley mounted on her hip, Delia opened the door for him and he set the water on the counter top. "What's this?" Delia asked. Hadley reached out and fingered the top of one of the jugs.

"Just heard that the water treatment plant's in danger."

"We'll have no water? How will I bathe Hadley?"

"The least of your worries if the plant floods," he said.

Delia sighed. She looked up at the kitchen ceiling. "Enough, God." Then she kissed Andy on the mouth. "You're too wonderful. The way you take care of me." She sometimes thought she should pinch herself, or maybe pinch Andy, to see if he was real.

Delia put Hadley in her high chair with some cheese cubes and bread sticks, then set the dinner on the table. After they ate their fried chicken and potato salad, Andy got up, stood by the open door, and lit up a Camel. As far as Delia could tell, it was his only vice. They were unfiltered cigarettes, but he only smoked four or five a day, and even though Delia had quit three years ago, it didn't really bother her—as long as the smoke didn't go anywhere near Hadley.

"Are you sure you don't want me to call my niece?" Andy said, blowing the smoke out into the garage. He and Delia had plans to go bowling with a group Andy had been bowling with for years.

"Hadley isn't used to sitters," Delia explained.

"She's fourteen and very responsible. An A student, on the volleyball team, doesn't date," Andy tried.

"I'd never be able to enjoy myself," Delia said. "I'd just be a nervous wreck."

While Delia secured Hadley into the car and handed her her pacifier, Andy went out into the driveway and stared up at the sky. The rain had let up and was now a heavy mist. "The clouds are rolling off to the northeast," Andy said. "We may even see the sun tomorrow."

"Then we'll have the steambath," Delia said as she joined him in the driveway. She did not mean that she would not welcome the sun. In fact, she imagined that if indeed it happened, she would set the little wading pool in the backyard, and while Hadley splashed around in four inches of water, she would sit in a lawn-chair to read the magazines—*People, House & Garden, Mirabella*—

that her sister Ginny saved for her. At the same time, she knew from past experience that there was so much moisture in the ground that whenever the sun did make even a brief appearance, the steam rose from every tiny pore in the earth.

When Andy put his arm around Delia she leaned into him and closed her eyes. Andy felt solid, secure, and Delia felt very, very lucky that her friend Rosalie, who worked with her at Allied, had introduced them. They met at a downtown bar called One-Eyed Jake's well before the rains came and two days before Stacey was released from drug rehab. It was Rosalie's birthday, and a group from the office was celebrating with beer and brats. Andy appeared after work, too, with some men from his crew at the phone company. He was playing pool when Rosalie, who'd already had a few beers, spotted him and shouted across the room. "Andeee!" After he finished making his shot, he came over to the table, and Rosalie introduced them. "My third cousin, twice removed. Isn't that right, Andy?"

Looking directly at Delia, Andy smiled. "Close enough," he said. In high spirits that evening and with Hadley safely in the care of her sister Ginny, Delia was full of hope that she and Stacey would mend, so when she eyed Andy that first time, she felt as though she were floating on a breeze.

"It was fate that we met," Andy said into the drizzling rain.

"I was just thinking about that night myself," she said.

Andy pulled her a little closer to him. "I was watching you, and thinking, 'That woman knows something I want to know.'"

Delia pulled away, looked into the side of his face. "You're kidding."

"You were completely at ease. And funny."

She laughed. "I'm a cheap drunk, remember? Two beers is all I need. Besides, I really believed Stacey was coming home for good."

Andy held onto her again.

"God, Andy. Where is she?"

"She's learning what she has to learn, Delia."

She knew this was meant to comfort her, but it didn't. "And now you think I'm no fun at all," Delia said.

"I know it's still in there," said Andy, tilting his head up toward the troubled sky. "And I'm a very patient man."

It was just after 7:30, and for the first time all week the children in Delia's neighborhood were outside skateboarding along the sidewalk, playing hopscotch, jumping rope, shrieking and running around. One little girl, a wiry nine-year-old with a wheat-colored ponytail, was doing cartwheels over the wet lawn across the street, and for an instant Delia thought that it was Stacey. Stacey, who at nine dreamed of becoming an Olympic gymnast, who at nine used to dump her mother's beer down the kitchen sink, break up and toss her mother's cigarettes into the toilet.

Delia squeezed her eyes shut again and wrapped both her arms around Andy's middle, but there was always that little kernel of fear that bounced aimlessly around inside her, saying it was too good to last. After all, Stacey's father Ray was a drunk, and Errol, the second one after Ray, was an abuser. Delia still had trouble admitting that it was when Errol came to live with them that Stacey took a bad turn.

Hadley was crying. "Oh God," Delia said.

"It won't hurt her to cry for thirty seconds," said Andy, but Delia did not hear him.

"Stacey," she called, hurrying to the car.

Delia was in the driver's seat and had already started the car when Andy climbed in next to her. "You called Hadley Stacey," he said.

Delia stared at him, his eyebrows arched in accusation. "You drive," she said. She quickly handed him the keys, walked around to the other side of the car, and got in.

Andy backed out of the driveway, but Delia hardly noticed. She was thinking about an argument she'd had with Stacey about three weeks before Stacey disappeared. Delia had been awakened out of a deep sleep a little after three in the morning by the sound of Hadley's crying. She lay there staring up at the ceiling, waiting for the crying to stop, and when it didn't, she was afraid Stacey had gone out after midnight like she sometimes did, so she went to Stacey and Hadley's room to check. As soon as she opened the door, Hadley stopped crying and sat up.

"Can't you knock?" Stacey said.

"I thought you weren't here."

"You saw me go to bed."

"But sometimes . . ."

"You can knock."

Hadley started crying again.

"Aren't you going to pick her up?" Delia asked.

Stacey had turned her own face toward the wall, away from both Delia and Hadley. "No. I'm not," she said.

By this time Hadley was howling.

"She wants you to pick her up, Stacey."

"Please. Delia. Please just leave."

Delia stood in the doorway.

"She's old enough to sleep through the night," Stacey said into the wall. "All the books say so. The pediatrician says let her cry."

"For God's sake, Stacey, she's a little baby."

"She's my little baby," Stacey said.

Not wanting to remember the rest, Delia turned and focused on Hadley who seemed content now, rhythmically sucking at her pacifier in the back seat. As Andy drove on down the street, past the pony-tailed, cartwheel-turning girl, past the elementary school on the corner, Delia looked over at him and said, "I'm sorry, Andy."

"Sorry for what?"

"For being a party pooper," she said. Then she laughed nervously, realizing that such language aged her.

Andy reached over and affectionately patted her left knee while Delia looked out the passenger's window, staring at what she believed was a Stacey flyer taped onto the plate-glass window of the drugstore.

At the bowling alley, she felt a momentary freedom in the crowd. They ordered pitchers of beer, and she drank three mugs full. Frightened by the endless rain, they told flood jokes; they bowled three games. Her first earned a score of 152, but with each mug of beer, her score went down. In the eighth frame of the third game she even threw a gutter ball. "Get out the bumper cushions," she shrieked. These were Andy's friends watching her, and she looked back at Andy who viewed her animated silliness with a proud grin. Despite the thundering balls, the crashing pins, the typical uproar inside a bowling alley, Hadley was asleep in her stroller, and all was well with Delia.

A few hours later, inside Delia's bedroom, Andy had just begun to move his hand slowly over the inside of Delia's thigh. The rain had returned and was battering the window on the west side of the room. Delia was thinking, *There is nowhere for all this water to go.* It surprised her that she was not afraid, even for Stacey; not while Andy was making her want him. "We have all night," he whispered to her, while his hands moved over her in slow motion. She was transported away from all that terrified her so that when Hadley cried, it was actually Andy who heard her first, and he crossed his leg over hers, telling Delia not to get up. They were both calling her at once; they each had an arm and were yanking at her. As Hadley's cries grew stronger, Delia slid out from under Andy and went to her while the rain poured out of the black sky.

Two weeks went by and the rain had not let up. There were pauses when the sun broke through the clouds, but these were rare. Another round of dark skies usually followed, rumbling like distant drums, flickering like blinking strobes, suddenly opening up and releasing the Niagara over the Midwest. All along the Mississippi there were floods; cities as large as Davenport and towns as small as Chelsea in eastern Iowa were submerged. In the middle of Iowa, where Delia and Hadley lived, the Des Moines and Raccoon rivers poured over their banks and became an inland ocean. The water treatment plant flooded and had to be shut down, and Delia, along with many thousands of other city residents, no longer had tap water.

The phone company was more than two weeks behind in answering its repair calls, and Andy continued to work ten, twelve, sometimes fourteen hours a day. Delia, meanwhile, was back at her job at Allied, and Hadley was just beginning to adjust to the Little People Daycare Center.

Tensions in the city ran high. The people were only a few days without water, but already there were groans about greasy hair and overflowing baskets of dirty laundry. Delia was one of the fortunate ones. She knew it was coming. Even the mayor did not believe it would happen. With Andy's warning, Delia had filled every jug, plastic milk carton, Tupperware container, and jar she could find. Every morning before she left for work, she filled the bathtub. And of course she had the drinking water Andy had brought her.

So far Hadley had not suffered. Delia had several boxes of Pampers and enough clean clothes for Hadley to get through another week. To daycare everyday, she sent two plastic baby bottles of purified water with Hadley's name clearly taped onto the front.

Sitting at her desk at Allied, Delia looked at her watch—10:15, break time—then stared at the photo of Hadley, recently taken at Sears, which was just to the right of her PC monitor. This was just about the time Hadley got fussy and needed to be carried around before she was sleepy enough to take her morning nap. Delia told this to the staff at Little People several times, but they always gave her the same answer. "She's doing fine."

This was not specific enough for Delia. Delia was sending Hadley off into the unknown and wanted a blow-by-blow account of Hadley's day. More than that, she needed to know that there weren't any weirdos working at the daycare. Every week now it seemed that another childcare worker, another babysitter somewhere, harmed a child. Two days ago, when Delia brought Hadley home and undressed her, checking for suspicious marks, she found a dime-sized blue bruise on Hadley's knee, a bruise for which the staff at Little People could give no explanation.

Instead of going to the break room for coffee, Delia headed for the Ladies' and then back to her desk where she called Detective Holtzman. John Holtzman was with Missing Persons and in charge of Stacey's file. Delia had still not heard a word from Stacey, and she alternated between anger and anguish. The last time Stacey left, even though she would not tell Delia where she was, she phoned every ten days or so. This time, Stacey had not phoned once, though there had been several questionable hang-ups on Delia's answering machine.

"Holtzman here."

"It's Delia about Stacey. I haven't talked to you for a few days now, and ..."

"Nothing new, Delia. I would phone you the minute ..."

"What if she's dead?" Delia said. Though she thought it many times, it was the first time she said the word out loud. Dead. When the city flooded, Delia began seeing the recurring image of Stacey lying face down in water.

"Delia," Holtzman said, "if we get a report of an unidentified woman anywhere, we check everyone in our file who might be a match."

Delia knew that Holtzman was impatient with her, that he didn't take Stacey's leaving seriously because Stacey had left before. But what if Stacey was not a runaway this time? What if she'd been kidnapped, Delia thought. She knew that Stacey was last seen getting into the back of a black Pontiac Trans Am, which was driven by a dark-haired, pony-tailed, tattooed, earringed young man in his twenties. Delia knew from Stacey's troubled friends that this was the same man Stacey had been seen with many times before, as far back as when she was five or six months pregnant, though he was clearly not Hadley's father. Hadley's father was blond and preppie-looking (though he, too, took a variety of drugs).

"What about all those shelters they have for kids?" Delia said. "Like in Seattle. Or Minneapolis. Or LA."

"I know how upsetting this is for you, Delia," Holtzman said. "The waiting is unbearable. But they usually call. Eventually they do."

Delia thought him patronizing and hung up before he could say more, but she knew she didn't hate him. A moment later the phone rang. "Billing," she said.

"Guess where we're going for your birthday tomorrow?" Andy asked.

"But it's not till next Wednesday." She was turning forty and could hardly believe it, even though Ginny insisted that forty was the best number to be.

"I know your birthday's Wednesday, but tomorrow I have the whole day off and I want to take you to Tama. Blackjack, roulette, poker, Meskwaki Bingo, you name the game," he said.

She looked over at Hadley's picture. She was smiling and clutching a pink stuffed bunny. Delia knew she'd talked with Andy about going to Tama, but that was long before Stacey left. "But Hadley," she said.

"It's all arranged. My sister and my niece."

But Delia had never met Andy's niece and only talked to his sister once, for five minutes. Her heart was pounding. How could she leave Hadley with perfect strangers?

"Delia?" Andy said.

"I'm thinking, I'm thinking. I can get one of those backpacks, wear Hadley on my back."

"I don't think they let kids in," Andy said.

"But she's a baby," said Delia. "She's just a little baby."

"Can't you leave her just this once?"

He was pleading, she could hear it in his voice, and she feared losing him, but she knew she just couldn't leave Hadley on a Saturday, not when she had to leave her at the daycare Monday through Friday.

Andy was kind enough to celebrate Delia's birthday anyway. He agreed to just what Delia wanted. Instead of going to the

Meskwaki Settlement to play blackjack, they drove twenty miles west out of the city and, just off the interstate, they got a room at the Ramada. The city water supply was still shut down (the water treatment plant was now sitting on what had become a spit of an island), and at the hotel they could take showers, wash their hair, give Hadley a bath, do their laundry, swim in the hotel pool. It was raining once again of course, but the Ramada had an indoor pool.

They spent the day under water. Whenever Hadley was napping, they got in the shower again. Ahh, hot running water. Hair that squeaked. In the days of the big midwestern flood, squeaky hair was a luxury. Andy shampooed Delia's hair, massaging her scalp with the tips of his fingers. "You're good enough to work in a salon," she said, smiling.

When he smiled back, Delia wanted to think of the three of them as a family, yet she knew that something was terribly wrong. After the hot shower, they made sure Hadley was still sleeping before they climbed between the crisp, clean sheets to make quiet love. This was when Delia knew for certain that something had changed, that as they went through the motions—and it was just that, going through the motions—something irreparable had happened.

That evening they had dinner in the hotel dining room. Andy would have preferred a different restaurant, but as Delia pointed out, they were just off the interstate and would have to drive back to the city, where there was no water, to get a better meal. Trooper that he was though, Andy tried to make it special by ordering champagne, and Hadley almost made it through the entire meal before she got antsy and wanted to move around. When she started banging her spoon on the metal tray of the high chair, Andy said, "Let her out. She can crawl around on the floor under the table."

Delia looked down at the bread crumbs sprinkled on the patterned carpet. "It's dirty," she said. "Who knows all the feet that were under here?"

Andy finished his champagne about the same time that Hadley started to whine. Her whine soon turned into a shriek, which forced Delia to take her out of the high chair and set her on her lap. In a flash and before Delia could prevent it, Hadley grabbed the stem of the champagne glass and knocked it over, spilling the contents onto the red tablecloth. Delia looked at

Andy, and for the first time she saw that he had lost his patience. "I guess I should take her back up to the room," she said. But she felt that little ball of electrified panic bobbing around inside her.

Andy said nothing; he stared at the dark spill on the table.

"Oh, God, Andy, I'm sorry. You hate me, don't you?"

He blotted his mouth on a napkin. "Delia," he said. "You think I don't understand what you're going through with Stacey, but I do."

"You never really liked her, did you?"

Hadley picked up Delia's fork and began tapping it on the edge of the table.

"I didn't really get to know Stacey," he said. "She wouldn't let me."

"I know how hard this is for you, Andy."

"I don't know what else I can do, Delia."

When Hadley yanked at the hem of the tablecloth, Delia pushed back her chair, stood up, and shifted Hadley onto her hip. "I should get her out of here," she said.

"Mum, mum, mum, mum," Hadley said, affectionately patting Delia's cheek. For the past week or so, Hadley had been calling Delia Mumma.

Andy was looking at his fingernails. Delia looked from Hadley to Andy and back to Hadley. The magnet was pulling at her from both poles, but in the end she knew which pole had the greater force.

"See you upstairs?" Delia said.

Andy nodded but he still wasn't looking at her. He took his napkin off his lap, folded it neatly, and laid it on the table. Then he stared across the room toward the swinging doors that led into the restaurant's kitchen.

Delia began to walk away. *He can't understand that Hadley has no one else but me.* And Hadley cooed into her ear, probing her tiny fingers into the corner of Delia's mouth. "Mumma," she said.

They were almost out of the restaurant when Delia saw the candles flickering atop the birthday cake as the waitress carried it across the room toward the table where Andy now sat alone. She wanted to go back, sit down at the table, take Andy's hand and squeeze it, but the magnetic force was still pulling at her, sucking her and Hadley out the door. By the time she reached the motel lobby, she knew she would have to let Andy go.

Though the water treatment plant was finally operating at full service, Delia was still overly cautious. She boiled water for Hadley in her stainless-steel tea kettle every morning now before she went to work. As she waited for the kettle to whistle, she sipped at her coffee and listened for Hadley. She found that mornings were the worst time, even though it was now three weeks since she'd had to give Andy up. Her heart still felt heavy with loss, but she knew there was nothing she could do. And, as she explained to Andy, it was really no one's fault.

But Delia was determined to go on. She knew she must, for Hadley's sake. Amazingly, she had energy. She had even taken care of some things she had meant to do a year ago. She refinanced her house, for instance. When she bought the house ten years ago (a year or so before Errol), interest rates were sky high, and now they were so low that she could refinance. She could save so much on her monthly payment that she asked Allied if they would let her work thirty-two hours instead of forty so she could have Fridays off to spend more time with Hadley. She knew her budget would be a little tight, but it would only be a few years before Hadley was in school. She could go back full-time then and use the extra money to start a savings account so Hadley could go off to Iowa State and get herself a good career job, maybe become a veterinarian or something else scientific. She certainly didn't want her to end up as a billing clerk at Allied.

At 10:15 that morning, Delia poured coffee in the break room, then went to the window and looked out at the falling rain. After a let-up of more than a week, the city was under siege once again. The break room was on the fifth floor, and Delia looked down at the street, watching a man in a grey suit, a black umbrella raised over his head, step down off the sidewalk into a pool of murky water. Carrying her coffee back to her desk, she imagined Stacey and her ponytailed boyfriend standing on a street corner, begging in the rain.

At 10:20, she phoned Detective Holtzman as she did now every Monday and Thursday.

"Hi, Delia," he said, even before she announced herself.

"Anything today?" she asked.

She expected to hear the familiar, "Sorry, Delia." Instead he said, "Last night . . ."

"What?"

"We're still checking it out."

She felt a pulse thumping in the side of her neck. "What are you saying?"

"It might be nothing, but we got a phone call last night and we think he was asking about Stacey."

"Oh, God," Delia said. "He could be a kidnapper."

"Listen, Delia. We're checking it out, and we want you to come down sometime this afternoon."

"Where did he call from?" Delia wanted to know.

"We're talking to Minneapolis right now."

"She was there all this time?" Delia felt the sweat collecting under her arms and didn't notice that her supervisor was standing at the side of her desk.

"Can you come down after work?" he said. "We'll know something then."

"As soon as I pick up Hadley."

When Delia hung up she was in a fog, but she went into the computer files and pulled up the record Fran, her supervisor, had asked for. "He's rear-ended somebody," Fran said. "And forgot to pay his premium."

Delia stared at the words and numbers on the computer screen, but she was thinking about all the times the phone had rung at home in the evening and when she had answered it, no one was on the line.

By the time she got to Holtzman's office, Delia was frantic, though for Hadley's sake, she tried to stay calm. Holtzman pointed to the chair at the side of his desk, and she sat down. Because Hadley could now stand up and walk while holding onto things, Delia let her totter around the one remaining chair. Meanwhile, Holtzman had his hand on Delia's shoulder, and Delia noticed for the first time that Holtzman had sideburns. She almost said something to him: *So, I see that men are wearing sideburns once again.* Instead, she looked into his eyes, trying to read what he was about to tell her—that Stacey was dead?—but his face blurred, and for an instant she thought he was Andy and that he would comfort her, that together they would be a family. "It's okay, Delia," Holtzman said. "It's definitely not Stacey. We got word half an hour ago."

She couldn't stop shaking. Her teeth were chattering.

"The description matched, but the dental records don't," he

said. "Remember? You gave me permission weeks ago to get Stacey's dental records."

She nodded, but she was in shock. As frightened as she'd been all day, it hadn't registered that they were talking about a body. Maybe Stacey's body. Her daughter Stacey who started smoking cigarettes at twelve, marijuana at thirteen. As she allowed the words to sink in, as she got heavier and heavier in her chair, she could hardly see Hadley as she tried to make it from the chair to the metal filing cabinet where she slipped and fell and struck her forehead just above the right eyebrow on the corner of the bottom drawer, which was open less than an inch. She did notice that Holtzman saw it first, the frantic child trying to get up, the blood running down over her eye, and he lept up out of his chair and lifted Hadley up off the floor before Delia could move even one heavy limb.

There was a lot of blood but by the time they got to the hospital, Delia was relieved that the wound would need only three little stitches. Yet she was consumed with guilt and could hardly bear to watch as they placed Hadley on a flat board and belted her flailing arms and legs. Hadley screamed, and once she looked up with a boiling rage in her eyes (they were Stacey's eyes) at Delia, who was powerless to help her.

After the stitches, Delia drove her home, and Hadley, just as the doctor said she would, fell soundly asleep in the car. Even when Delia carried her into the house, washed her, and changed her diaper, she did not awaken. Delia wanted to feed her some supper, but Hadley wanted to sleep off her trauma, and Delia had no choice but to put her to bed.

In the living room she turned on the TV and stared at it until it was dark. She got in bed, but the house smelled musty and she began to imagine the dangerous molds that were surely growing in every corner of every room. After an hour or so, she got up to check on Hadley. Except for a flutter of eyelashes, the little girl had not moved, despite the gauze patch that covered one side of her forehead. For a moment Delia stood over her, fearfully watching, and then she turned back the covers on Stacey's bed and climbed in for the night.

It was Delia who insisted that her sister Ginny make the appointment for the psychic reading. At first Ginny was reluctant, even though Ginny had been telling Delia for the past year that the psychic, a woman named Betty Bodine, was middle-class and mainstream and did the readings in the back of her yarn shop. "She's a knitter," Ginny had said.

After a bit of prodding from Delia, Ginny finally arranged a Saturday afternoon reading, and they went off together—Ginny, Delia, and Hadley, of course. Delia agreed to let Ginny take care of Hadley during the reading, and Ginny agreed that she would simply walk Hadley around the neighborhood in her stroller.

Betty Bodine had short wavy silver-blond hair and was wearing a pair of pale yellow cotton slacks and a white, handknit, short-sleeved, cotton sweater with some beadwork at the neckline. A young grandmother, thought Delia, as Betty escorted her to the back of the yarn shop where there was an office with a desk, a computer, and a swivel chair on one side of the room, and two flowered armchairs on the other side. As Betty motioned for her to sit in one of the armchairs, Delia noticed that all four walls were marked with a line two feet up from the floor. "You were flooded," Delia said when Betty sat down across from her.

"We had birch paneling in here," Betty told her. "We had to rip it out. We've bleached and we've painted, but still we can't cover it."

"I was lucky," Delia said. "The most I had was two inches in the basement."

Betty smiled. "Let's hope we've seen the end of it."

They sat together in a moment of silence, and Delia, unable to remember why she was there, wanted to get up and leave. Finally, she said, "I've never been to a fortune teller before."

In a steady but firm voice, Betty said, "I'm not a fortune teller and I don't make predictions because I'm a firm believer in the power of the will. Whatever I might see out there, you always have the will to overcome it."

"What do you already know about me?" Delia asked. She was suspicious and wondered what Ginny had revealed about her. But Betty simply closed her eyes, and soon she was taking deep breaths through her nose and exhaling through her mouth. She repeated this several times while Delia sat uncomfortably across from her. She saw Betty drop her head, her chin resting on her chest, and when she didn't move for a full minute or two, Delia was overcome by a terrible grief. Where did she go wrong, she wanted to know, when she saw an eight-year-old Stacey singing and jumping rope on the sidewalk in front of the house.

Then Betty suddenly lifted her head, opened her eyes, and began speaking in what Delia heard as an Irish brogue.

"You do live a paradox," Betty said.

Delia was amazed because Betty no longer sounded or looked like Betty. She had become a serious Irish woman in her mid-thirties.

"You are in turmoil."

Delia began to protest. "I am not."

But Betty didn't seem to hear. "You are in transition," she said.

But Delia sat across from Betty barely listening. Stacey was suddenly fourteen and stoned on marijuana, screaming at Delia's boyfriend Errol. Then fifteen and drunk in her room. Then seventeen and sitting in Delia's oak rocker, soothing an eight-pound Hadley, rocking, rocking, then looking up at Delia to say, "I love her so much." Then seventeen-and-a-half in the drug rehab center, sitting on the edge of a lower bunk, fury clenched in her jaw, refusing to look at the Polaroids of Hadley that Delia had brought to show her.

"You may change course several times, but you will find your way," she heard Betty say. To banish Stacey from her mind, Delia repeated the word "several" over and over in her head trying to roll her r's off the end of her tongue the way Betty was doing, and thought about what she would say to Ginny forty-five minutes from now. "What hocus-pocus. Honest to God, Ginny, the woman couldn't even get a bit part in one of those Brit movies." Which is when Ginny would say, "But it was your idea, Delia."

Betty continued, but Delia hardly heard a word of it, she was so put off by the fake accent. But she decided to be polite; she did not want to hurt the woman's feelings. Then it was over and Betty asked Delia if she had questions. Delia thought of testing the woman, asking her where she worked, who she lived with, if she had a man in her life, but she surprised herself when she looked straight at Betty and said, "My daughter Stacey. I want to know about my Stacey."

She saw Betty hesitate, drop her chin to her chest again, take several deep breaths. "There is great pain for both of you," Betty said. "She wants to return to you, but she cannot. She is afraid."

"She's alive, then," Delia said.

Betty closed her eyes. "She is somewhere where it is hot and dry."

Delia sat in the flowered-fabric-covered chair, quaking, terrified that something had happened to Hadley. Her heart pounded, her palms grew sweaty. *I must run out of the yarn shop, find Ginny and Hadley.*

"What else do you want to know?" Betty asked.

But there was nothing.

While Hadley napped, Delia stood in the kitchen and squeezed flowers from the corner of a plastic sandwich bag full of pink frosting onto the top of a chocolate layer cake. With green frosting, she drew curvy stems and a few petals for each pink flower, and with blue she wrote *Happy First Birthday Hadley*. She slid a two-inch candle into the center of the cake, then stood a few feet back to admire her work.

The guests were set to arrive at five for hotdogs, hamburgers, macaroni salad, cake, and ice cream. Of course, Delia knew that Hadley had no idea what a birthday was, though she might sense that the party was for her. Then, too, the guests were not exactly Hadley's friends; they were Delia's—Ginny, Ginny's daughter Alison, Rosalie and Charlene from Allied, and a single mother Bonnie and her three-year-old son Randy from the daycare center.

Delia had prepared well in advance: the balloons were blown, the camera was loaded with film, the hamburger patties were made, the macaroni salad was in the fridge, the table was set, the cake was decorated. This gave Delia another forty minutes or so to rest before Hadley woke up, so she went into the living room and lay down on the couch, but when she started to doze off, Stacey was standing over her. As soon as she saw her daughter's face, she knew right away that Stacey was in labor. For months Delia had been denying the pregnancy: Her daughter was too young to be a mother, and she was too young to be a grandmother. But Stacey, for the first time in years, needed her, and she got up and motioned for Stacey to sit down beside her on the couch. Gently she massaged Stacey's lower back. An hour later she drove her to the hospital and after eight more hours of labor, some of it very intense, Hadley was born. Stacey was exhausted and almost in a daze, and the doctor looked over at Delia and handed the baby to her.

Delia's eyes snapped open as she shifted her weight on the couch and tried to control her mounting anxiety. Instead of Hadley's birth she tried to think about the birthday party and what Hadley would do when she opened the handsewn rag doll, one of the gifts Delia had bought for her, but the bubble of fear that had lodged between her shoulder blades would not let go. Soon she heard Hadley's cries and rose up off the couch. The house, still swollen from the summer rains, was musty, cobweb-by, filled with noxious molds. By the time she reached her, Hadley was standing at the bars of her crib howling. Her face was flushed, her hair was damp, and when Delia felt the back of her neck, she was hot. A fever. She picked her up, cuddled her, patted her on the back. "Is my baby sick?" she cooed. "Poor Hadley. Gramma will make everything okay."

But Hadley could not be comforted, and she kept crying, something she rarely did when Delia carried her. Delia started out of the bedroom toward the bathroom to find the thermometer when Hadley suddenly stopped crying, lifted her head, and cocked her ear. Snowball barreled down the hallway and then Delia heard the phone ringing. She carried Hadley toward it, and they both felt it, the pull down the hallway toward the phone ringing in the kitchen. Delia felt herself moving slowly through a relentless humidity, a thick, warm fog. By the time she got to the kitchen, Snowball was meowing loudly, racing round and round Delia's feet. Hadley was jumping up and down in Delia's arms. As Delia picked up the phone, Hadley reached out and grabbed it, pulled it to her face and began to babble into the mouthpiece, "Mum, mum, mumma."

Vigil

Judith Bell

Iris stared at her television screen, looking for some piece of Trudy in these characters' lives. One woman was taking her husband back after he had run off for no good reason. Another, a photographer, fretted over a house painter ten years younger than her. None of this sounded like Trudy. She wished she could turn to Roy, ask what he thought, the way she seemed to do whenever she watched television now. But he'd been in bed for an hour, the old habit of turning in early for work still with him.

Thirty-eight years it'd been since she went to bed the same time as Roy. Before Trudy was born she had trailed to bed right behind him. He would either drop right off to sleep or do so soon after making love to her. Left alone, Iris would lie there staring into the dark, her body wound tight as a clock.

As a young girl she had stayed up as late as she possibly could without paying for it the next morning. Reading, or just looking into the dark outside her window, she closed off Gladys's even breathing on the other side of the room, pretending she had the world to herself. She couldn't bring herself to do that with Roy. If he was sleeping, she felt like she had no business being awake. It had something to do with her ideas about being a couple. But once Trudy came, she had all the reason she needed to be up late and at all hours. By the time Trudy had worked her way past night feedings then night wakings and nightmares, Roy had forgotten all about her coming to bed when he did. And then when Trudy was older she stayed up keeping Iris company, as much a night owl as she was. Now it was just Iris bumping around the house—had been for the nearly twenty years since Trudy left for college.

At the commercial she sat back in the big swivel rocker, exhausted. Trudy was no closer; still in Washington, D.C., and more than a thousand miles away, carrying on a life she didn't understand. "Washington is not Anamosa, Mama," Trudy responded the last time Iris called to complain about how long it'd been since she'd had a card or a call. "Watch the reruns of 'Thirtysomething.' You might learn something about my life since you don't seem to have the slightest idea what it's like."

"Hatefulest gal I ever saw," that was what Mama had said about Trudy when she was no more than four years old. Roy's father had died and Iris left Trudy at Mama's while she and Roy stayed with his mother the night before the funeral. Mama gave Trudy one of the barn kittens to sleep with and Trudy shut the little thing up in Iris's honeymoon suitcase—the good Samsonite Trudy had insisted she be allowed to pack. Terrified, the kitten relieved itself all over the beige rayon lining.

The next day, Trudy sat on the front steps the whole time, her clothes in a paper sack, the ammonia-infused suitcase open to the sun. Crying and watching for Iris, she refused both food and comfort. When they came to pick her up, she batted Iris's hands away and glared at her over Roy's shoulder as he carried her to the car. The whole drive home Iris felt Trudy's stare trained on her from the back seat, the eyes black as the fields they sped past, daring her mother to leave her again. "When I'm as old as you, will you be dead?" Trudy asked suddenly. Iris reached back to pat Trudy's leg, but the child pulled it under her skirt. "No, no, of course not. Mommy won't leave you."

And that was the first and last time Iris did. But somewhere along the way Trudy had changed her challenge, making it so Iris couldn't get close to her, know anything about her. Now this TV program felt like a secret, something Trudy had let slip in a moment of anger. Iris had watched it for months but she knew better than to let on that she had.

She remembered the time she was vacuuming the floor of the closet in Trudy's room. The probing wand of the vacuum overturned one of Trudy's buckskin boots and a slim blue aerosol can rolled to Iris's feet. She didn't have to pick it up to know what it was. Didn't she have a can just like it in the back of the bathroom cabinet hidden beneath the towels? She swept up the contraceptive foam, deposited it in the boot, smoothed the fringe that ran down the back of the leg. They were the boots Trudy wore on Saturday nights when she went out with her girlfriends. Just sixteen, she didn't even have a steady boyfriend. Maybe this foam was like the rubbers her friend Virginia Feezor had found in her boys' wallets, the writing on the wrappers worn thin as their hope of using them. Iris hurried through her cleaning, anxious to lie down and nurse the piercing headache starting behind her right eye. "Taking things out on yourself again," her sister Gladys would say if she saw her now. "Maybe this time I'll talk to Trudy," she had said out loud, more to chase her sister's voice from her throbbing head than for her own benefit. What Iris remembered doing instead was quietly counting the tampons Trudy insisted on using, making sure their number continued to dwindle each month.

All she knew about Trudy was her schedule, her deadlines—that was how she talked about her life. As near as she could tell, her schedule had a lot to do with her and her husband Phil living apart. The boys spent three weeks with Trudy, then three with Phil. Vesta, the babysitter from South America, shuttled back and forth between the house and the apartment Phil bought in the neighborhood.

Two of women on the show were talking about their husbands. "You think you know him," the blonde was saying. "I promise you, he will do something or reveal something that will rock you to the bottom of your soul." Why was there all this questioning, their words long and confusing as a doctor's? What had happened to taking things as they come? Maybe Phil had done something like that, to make Trudy rearrange their lives, something she was hiding from Iris.

Before Phil, Trudy, skirting thirty and still single, had suddenly began carrying on like she had run out of choices. She was thirty-one when she married Phil, long after Iris had thought there was any hope. The whole thing was sudden. First Trudy called saying she'd met this man, an attorney, and not four months later she sent her and Roy the plane tickets to come to the wedding.

It was November, a bad time for a wedding. Things were finishing, not beginning. A soft drizzle fell outside, darkening the interior of the church. Watching Trudy and Phil at the altar of a church neither one of them belonged to, Iris stared at Phil's back, the side of his face, when he turned to speak his vows. Nobody but Trudy could see him straight on, but from where Iris sat, he didn't seem sufficiently full of love. She kept seeing her own wedding and Roy choking on the words he repeated after their minister, his whole face lit up with joy.

Outside the rain changed, beat hard against the stained glass, drowning out Trudy and Phil's words. How could her daughter be spending the rest of her life with somebody Iris had just met over dinner the night before? Roy had come around two whole years before they decided to tie the knot, with Mama so used to him he walked right in the house without announcing himself. And even at that, Roy had called her mother Mrs. Jacobs right up to the day she died. "So, Iris," Phil had called her without asking if he could right after shaking her hand, "you and Roy are going to be family." He didn't have any of his own. His parents—well-to-do Easterners—were dead and the people on his side of the church were as young and strangely dressed as Trudy's friends. There was no one there she could study to see how he might age or how his temperament would settle.

All she had to go on was the place where he lived, the things he kept around him. Yesterday after Trudy met her and Roy at the airport and took them to their hotel, they had walked the four blocks to Phil's house. On the street Iris held fast to Roy's arm, the noise and size of things rattling her nerves.

"Wait until you see our house." Trudy talked above the roar of the traffic as she led them through the crowd of people making their way home from work. "It's right in the middle of gallery row."

"Is that good for your art?" Iris asked, struggling in her high heels to keep pace with Roy.

"No, but it's nice having other art people around."

Iris pretended interest in the storefronts they passed to hide her embarrassment. How could she have asked such a thing? Trudy was a performance artist. She had nothing to show and Iris knew Trudy thought she should know better.

"There's the restaurant where we'll be having dinner. It's northern Italian."

Iris started to ask what that meant but held her tongue, peering instead into the large glass windows overlooking the dining room. The tables were filled with men in dark suits and women in black. Waiters in tuxedos rushed between the crowded tables, some carrying baskets of broken loaves of bread. Iris pulled her coat closed over her turquoise dress. "I don't see any place to sit."

Trudy sighed; pausing, Iris imagined, to regain her patience before she spoke just the way she herself had once counted to ten when Trudy was little and getting on her nerves. "Don't worry, our reservation is for much later."

Trudy led them down a side street where the houses were stuck up side by side, their facades part of one long wall that went on as far as Iris could see. At first they looked the same but when she looked close, she saw that the doors were different, that the brick had been painted or left plain. Small things, touches you could see when you looked hard enough. And no two yards were alike. Instead of grass there were elevated flower beds, rocks piled in ways that looked intentional, ivy or other plants covering the ground. Trudy stopped in front of a house where the bare branches of a small tree drooped gracefully. "Cherry," Trudy said. "Phil put it in when he realized he never had time to get to the tidal basin to see the cherry blossoms."

Iris held out her hand, letting the bare branches drag across her palm. Even though it was winter she would enjoy seeing the cherry trees, the monuments by the river. Then she remembered how Trudy rolled her eyes and complained about tourists and thought better of suggesting it.

Trudy pulled a key on a long chain from inside her sweater and opened the heavy wooden door with the lion's head knocker. "My generation's answer to the high school ring," she said, dropping the key back inside her clothes. She led them up a short flight of stairs. "Sweetheart, we're home," she called out.

The sound of tenderness in Trudy's voice surprised Iris. Like the people in the restaurant, everything in the room was black—the leather couch and chairs, the tables, the floor lamps—except for the walls which were lacquered poppy red. On the black marble mantle a simple glass vase held a single red flower, its petals waxy like the walls. A black and white photograph of an angry looking young man in a leather jacket with a cigarette between his full lips stared down at her in defiance. She wondered if this was a picture of Phil.

"Sweetheart," she heard Phil answer Trudy, his voice coming from beyond the gray dining room. Iris strained to catch his words, to read the tone he used with her daughter, but his voice dropped to a murmur. Trudy giggled the way she had a habit of doing when she was nervous. She heard glass tinkling, the rattle of ice trays being opened. The familiar sound gave her the courage to steal a sideways glance at Roy.

"Don't look so worried," Roy said. "They just got a different way of doing things. We get him out our way, he'll be all right."

Maybe Roy was right. The place was so bare—sleek, Trudy

would say. There was something unforgiving about it. That couch, Iris just knew it'd be cold to the backs of her legs. And the red walls had her feeling anxious. She had heard on some talk show about experiments done with colors and prisoners, how their moods were affected by the color of the walls in their cells. Red was the worst; it made the men feel closed in, worked up. After seeing that show, she had painted her and Roy's room pale pink.

Phil glided into the room carrying a silver tray with some glasses and an ice bucket. Iris thought of a man's shoes as being substantial, like the wing tips Roy wore, but Phil's loafers looked as flimsy as slippers. His sweater was soft, luxurious like something a woman would wear. Light blonde stubble covered his face as though he'd forgotten to shave the last few days. His straight hair was pulled into a short pony tail at the nape of his neck. There was a tiny gold stud earring in his left earlobe. He didn't look like any lawyer Iris had ever seen. And he certainly didn't show any of the spunk of the boy in the picture over the mantle, or of the boys Trudy usually went for. Like something out of a magazine with their square jaws and thick hair. It was a dangerous thing when a man bested you in the looks department. Iris had seen Trudy desperate—her face swollen from crying, her voice nearly gone from yelling—enough times to know that men that good-looking broke your heart. With Phil, homely as Roy but without the starch Iris found so attractive, it looked like Trudy was finally broke of her habit.

"So, Iris." Phil took her hand, clasping it between his. "Your daughter's told me all about Iowa and about you and Roy."

His hands were cold like those of an old person who'd been still too long. She told herself it was working with the ice, handling the silver tray.

"I thought we'd start off with champagne." Iris watched Phil's hands twist the wire off the cork, wrap a white cloth napkin around the mouth of the bottle. His nails were clean and even, the skin around them smooth, unbroken. Maybe he was a lawyer after all.

"Phil's too modest," Trudy beamed. "He called everywhere until he found a bottle from 1945. The year you were married," she added when Iris gave her a blank look.

Iris couldn't see what her wedding date had to do with them, but she took the glass he handed her, watched the bubbles race toward the surface just like she'd seen them do in the commercials they ran around Christmas time.

"What shall we drink to?" Phil asked.

"Good luck'd be about right." Roy's big hand wrapped clear around the bowl of the delicate glass, the stem protruded from his fist.

Phil laughed and his whole face warmed. "Too late to call on luck. Let's drink to family."

He could laugh at himself, that was something. He tapped his glass against Roy's hand, Trudy's glass clinked against Iris's, and on they went until everybody's had touched everyone else's. Like turned cider, that was how the taste struck Iris.

Phil motioned them towards the couch and Trudy passed a plate of cheese and crackers. "Just the other day there was an article in the paper about a new cheese shop in Georgetown and I mentioned it to Phil, said we should try it sometime."

Why was Trudy's voice going up at the end of a sentence? Had she asked a question Iris missed?

Trudy sat on the arm of Phil's chair, draped her arm around his shoulder as though she had been doing it all her life. "He ran over there on his lunch hour today so we'd have something special to serve you." Phil puckered his lips in a kiss, prepared a cracker with cheese and fed it to Trudy.

Made uncomfortable by their exchange, Iris shifted her attention to the cheese platter. Shopping for cheese, nothing for a man to be doing. She could just imagine what Roy would come back with if she sent him off on such an errand. She didn't see anything that looked like American, the only kind of cheese she kept in her house. She placed a thin slice of the white triangle closest to her on a cracker—the same cheese Phil had chosen for Trudy—raised it to her mouth, then put it on the tiny black napkin Trudy handed her. How could Trudy serve something that smelled like a wet dog?

Closing her napkin over her cheese, Iris asked for the bathroom. Upstairs she walked by one, two, three bedrooms before she came to it. She had intended to flush the napkin, cheese and all. Her own feelings too hurt to worry about Trudy's, she tossed the whole business in the black metal wastebasket under the sink.

Back at the hotel, the ice machine across the hall ran all night long. A woman, laughing deep in her throat like she was up to no good, passed their door. Iris pulled the covers over her ears, careful to keep the sheet between her and the blanket. She kept seeing all those empty bedrooms in Phil's house. There had been no call for a hotel, no call at all.

Iris tiptoed down the hall to the bedroom to check on Roy. She pulled the blanket he'd kicked off back over his legs; he was always restless until she joined him. "Check the baby," he murmured, reaching out to pat her pillow. Roy worried about Trudy, too, though awake he'd never admit it. Iris thought of her mother at the end, carrying a baby doll around the nursing home, cradling the plastic head to her slack breast. Maybe the vigil of parenting, once acquired, stayed with you for life.

Iris hurried back to the den, turned the sound back up on the TV. Things had been fine for Trudy and Phil at first, making Iris think she had worried needlessly. That was until the children came along, and Phil proved himself to be as ungenerous as his furniture. Iris had gone to help Trudy right after she came home from the hospital with Halley, named for the comet that swung by the year he was born. Each night of her stay, she and Trudy ate their supper alone in the gray dining room, passing the crying baby between them while Trudy watched the clock, her face getting tighter as the minutes ticked away on the numberless dial. After the baby nursed for the last time and she and Trudy were both in bed, Iris heard the groan of the big wood door and Phil's step taking him to the bar just inside the dining room. Iris couldn't help but think of Roy and how he made a bee line for Trudy's room the moment he was in the house each night. Later, after she had fallen off to sleep, she heard them, Trudy and Phil, their voices firing across the broad expanse of their bedroom, each one accusing the other of not caring or doing enough. Where was the joy, she asked herself, the joy they should feel about the new life they had made?

"It's not as bad as it looks," Trudy had said at breakfast the next morning. "He's really good with Halley on the weekends when he has the time to be with him. It's just the work that makes things so difficult."

"Of course it is," Iris said, patting Trudy's hand, pushing aside her own doubts.

Phil kept right on working until all hours and Trudy complained she had to buy help to have any time of her own. But as bad as things were between them, Trudy was determined Halley wouldn't be an only child like her, like Phil. She had turned right around and had number two, and Samuel, bless his heart, had been the proverbial straw. Iris had heard those therapists and marriage counselors on Oprah say as much: nothing harder on a marriage than little children. Especially, Iris had thought to herself, when the husband and wife didn't have much interest in being grown-ups themselves.

When Trudy called to say that they had made different plans, that Phil was moving out, it was hard to feel any sense of loss. She could count on one hand the times she'd seen her son-in-law. Trudy always came alone with the children to visit. And when Iris and Roy had gone to Washington to see them, Phil had stayed late at the office and left before breakfast the next day. When he ran into them in the dining room or the hall outside the bathroom, he acted as surprised to see them as if they were plumbers or electricians who had shown up unexpectedly.

"So, Iris," he had said the last time she saw him in his own house, "I trust you're enjoying Washington." They were the same practiced words used by the clerk at the hotel where she and Roy stayed during the wedding. Phil adjusted his ponytail, a gesture that Iris now knew meant he was impatient to finish with her and get on to the next thing. Before she could answer, the beeper attached to his belt went off. Phil looked down at the flashing phone number. "Happens every time I turn the thing on before I get out of the house." He squeezed her arm, then bolted down the hall for the phone in the master bedroom. When Iris came out of the bathroom, she found Trudy alone and rocking a crying Halley so hard his head bobbed against her chest.

Separated—Iris didn't know what else to call it, even though Trudy said that wasn't the case, that they were simply living separately—Trudy and Phil got along better, going out to dinner with the boys or alone. On his own he had managed to find a way around his long work hours and Trudy finally felt she had enough time for herself and her work. What Iris didn't understand was why they couldn't work things out under the same roof. "We should have stayed lovers," Trudy had said, the contented tone in her voice making Iris think they still were. Why shouldn't Trudy feel satisfied? She had managed to get it all without being responsible for any of it: not her children, her house, or her lover. That left plenty of room for Trudy's art which was what she really studied.

Trudy called herself a performance artist. As far as Iris could tell, this meant there was nothing to see, no paintings or statues, the things regular people thought of when you said art. Roy's disinterest in personal things had paid off where it came to Trudy.

He never asked her about her art, or to see evidence of it, accepting instead the summarized and edited reports Iris gave him from Trudy's letters and newspaper clippings. Sometimes Iris went too far, telling too much. "I didn't send her to school for such as that," Roy would cry. "She studied being an actress, why isn't she on TV?" Iris would bite her tongue to keep from reminding him that Trudy had sent herself to school, that what she wanted to be was her own business.

Iris had figured out that what her daughter did was talk—trance-like, once she got going—in ill-fitting costumes that stood for something other than clothes. On stage Trudy went on about her private life mostly, or pretended to. When the papers mentioned things Trudy said, Iris had trouble figuring out where the truth left off and the make-believe began. Everything felt turned around, opened up, just the way it had when Trudy was little and she sensed the child was lying but had no proof.

There had been that time in the third grade when Iris got called down to the school because a boy in Trudy's class accused Trudy of tearing up his homework during recess. "I never *touched* his paper," Trudy said, looking from Iris to her teacher and back again, her face as fixed and even as the words framing her denial. A line of fluorescent lights split the length of hallway, pointing up the pilled surface of Trudy's sweater, the chalky line of dried milk on her upper lip. Surely if there was a fib in Trudy's face Iris would see it. The teacher nodded, pointed Trudy back toward the classroom. "I'm satisfied that's the end of it. They don't dare lie with a parent standing here." Iris had thanked the teacher for her trouble and hurried toward the red exit sign before the bare lights revealed her own uncertainty.

Reading the papers, she realized that whatever sure knowledge she had of Trudy left off somewhere around age fourteen. There were all those times in junior high that Trudy had gone with her best friend, Tammy, and her mother to the Faith Holiness Church where the members spoke in tongues, rolled in the very aisles, the women with their dress tails up over their heads. She should have kept her at home, or insisted Tammy come along to the First Baptist with them. The only time that congregation got out of their seats was to sing a hymn or to accept Christ as their savior.

But Trudy seemed to spend a lot more time planning her performances than she did doing them out in public. She passed the better part of her days on the third floor of her house in what she called her "contemplative space," while downstairs, if it was her three weeks for parenting, Vesta cleaned and watched the children once they got home from pre-school.

Cleaning. Iris didn't know what she would do without doing it. The daily scrubbing and scouring and polishing made life seem manageable, purposeful. She leaned forward, looked into her gleaming kitchen, feeling all its luster shoring her up for the world beyond this room. She'd said as much to Trudy once when they sat having coffee in Trudy's dining room while Vesta took apart the stove top for its weekly cleaning. "Hearing all that fuss and clatter makes me feel almost as good as doing it myself. Nothing like it to set you right."

Staring at the top of Trudy's dark head, waiting for her to look up from the morning paper, Iris suddenly saw Roy and all those mornings he sat ignoring her just this way, his mind on bigger things happening far off somewhere. Trudy was as wrapped up in herself as a man. The recognition hit her as hard as the wall she ran into whenever she tried talking to Roy about anything beyond the house or the car. When Trudy talked, it was about herself, her work, her source material: the goings on of the world told over and over in the newspapers and magazines she read, the news analysis shows she watched, the talk radio she listened to in the car. When Iris was Trudy's age she'd been so caught up with the house and taking care of Trudy she didn't have time for anything else. Roy, Trudy, doing for them had a way of eating up any time she might set aside for herself. Now Trudy was as stubborn about not being disturbed as she once had been about having Iris's undivided attention.

Iris tried to think of one time in the day that had been hers and all she came up with was the half hour between one thirty and two o'clock each week day when she watched her program, "As the World Turns." By then she had Trudy fed and down for a nap and Roy's lunch over with, if he'd bothered to come home from the Esso station he operated to eat it. But by the time Trudy was three—Samuel's age now—she'd given up daytime sleeping. When Iris tried to remember her half hour of rest, all she could see were Trudy's strong little hands, nails ribboned with dirt, digging into, pulling at her arms and legs, as she whined above the volume of the TV, reclaiming Iris for herself. Now Trudy called for Vesta when her own children interrupted her listening, reading, thinking.

Iris smoothed a scratch in the Naugahyde of the swivel rocker. She remembered how Trudy's family had lived before Vesta came. Halley was crawling, his hands and knees black from the dirty floor. You couldn't walk for the toys and the cracker crumbs. Trudy didn't seem to see any of it. The baby had the run of the house, putting God knows what in his mouth, while Trudy, pregnant, her studio relocated in the dining room so she wouldn't have to fight the stairs, poured over her books and magazines.

On the television the dark-haired one and her husband were in the same room talking on different phones, one of them a cordless. Their voices edged over each other and the babble of the toddler playing on the floor. Iris always worried about calling Trudy at the wrong time. She even had a page in the back of her phone book where she'd jotted down the times, the days, when she'd called and Trudy was on her way out the door, on the other line, or working in her studio. And when she and Phil were still living together, she had never liked calling after he was home. When he was there Trudy was vague, distracted by her husband's presence. It was as though she wished they'd all leave her alone: her mother, her husband, the boys. Except for Iris, Trudy had got her wish.

Sometimes she phoned and got the answering machine. Trudy's voice, sounding clipped and professional, told you what number you had reached and to please leave your message after the tone. Nobody Iris knew had these things. Listening to Trudy's taped voice, she imagined that her daughter was home, waiting to hear who was calling before she bothered to interrupt herself and pick up the phone.

"Call when you damned well please," Roy had barked when Iris fretted about disturbing Trudy. He clutched the arms of his chair where he spent his days; she noticed how thin the skin on the backs of his hands had grown. Too proud for a wheelchair, the swivel rocker was Roy's idea. From here he could watch her in the kitchen or moving around the table in the dining room. From across the room his hands looked black, the veins filled with old, tired blood. Drying up, that's what her mother would say about him if she were still living. He would be seventy-three on his next birthday. Iris turned over her own plump hands, studied the liver spots that resisted her nightly applications of Porcelaina. He was going to die first, her Roy who never once caught any of the colds and flus Trudy brought home from school. Iris had been the sick one, always running to the drugstore or the doctor. As she'd aged, things stayed the same with her; she got sick and then she got better. But Roy, ever since that flu last winter, had gone steadily downhill. Now he needed a cane or her arm for walking. He forgot things, what day it was, what she'd just said. Memories surfaced unsummoned, intruding on the present. There was a fear in him; she saw it when she held out her hand to help him to bed at night. He had slept deeply all his life but now he tossed and turned, waking in fits and starts, surprised and relieved to find himself still among the living. Failing. It was bound to be hard on somebody who'd never been sick, who'd never felt close to dying but this one time when it had to be the truth.

Iris could see how each decade gave some new hint of what was coming. First there had been the few gray hairs, the faint lines around the eyes, the weight that was harder to keep off. So far Trudy had outwitted all the normal changes. Slim as the day she finished high school, but muscled now, her upper arms and thighs resembling a young boy's, she did what she called working out. The last time they had visited, she left for her health club half-naked in an outfit skimpier than the bathing suits Iris remembered wearing at Trudy's age. Iris could remember thirty-eight. Her weight was up by then, the backs of her upper arms resting comfortably over her elbows, delicate arching lines running from her nose to her mouth, her blood pressure rising. Trudy still took stairs two at a time, her breath as regular as a child's. There were no lines in her face. She remembered summers at her mother's farm, Trudy brown as an Indian. Now Trudy coated her own children in sunscreen and was careful to apply it to herself every time she stepped outside. They were all pale; Trudy and the boys from her precautions, Phil from his long hours at his law practice.

Trudy did a lot of worrying. Not about the things that had tied Iris up in knots when she was her age—being a good wife and mother, keeping a clean house, looking after her parents, being a faithful Christian. She just seemed to think about herself, to get bogged down in all the things she could be doing if she weren't living the life she had. She just knew too much; and the knowing had got away with her.

Trudy complained to Phil about his working all the time. She had heard Trudy's demanding tone, as if she dared him to have something to say. But Phil was making good money. Weren't men supposed to work, to bring in the money? "Phil's in the middle of a big case," or "Phil is preparing for a trial," Trudy would say before the separation, her voice tight with some unnamed anger. She could remember when Trudy was a baby and Roy got an extra twenty dollars a week if he stayed late to close the service station every night. She'd been glad, glad to have the extra money. Maybe they hadn't had a lot of choices but at least everybody knew how they were supposed to act.

The last set of commercials came on the TV. Iris aimed the remote at the screen. She spun the chair around, studied the contents of the knotty pine shelves on either side of the picture window. The set of World Books she'd bought Trudy in junior high, the red Childcraft books she got her when she was three, were held up by the bookends decorated with her bronzed baby shoes. "Most folks bring in high tops for this," the shoe salesman had said doubtfully when she handed him the tiny pink satin shoes trimmed in lace and ribbons for bronzing. She didn't tell him so but she couldn't bear the thought of putting those ugly things on her baby. Now Trudy blamed Iris for her weak ankles. When she had her own boys, she had them wear specially prescribed doctor shoes for two years just to make sure their feet turned out right.

The shoes, the books. This old house was cramped, overflowing from a lifetime of holding onto things. Bought just two years after World War II with a GI loan, she'd loved the house for its picture windows, one front and back. Somewhere she read the idea for the windows had come from California; having two made her feel modern, up on things.

There had been a time—back when Trudy first went off to school on scholarship and the service station was finally Roy's—when she had thought of getting a house that was bigger, finer. Something she could spend her days fixing up the way her sister Gladys did when her and Dale bought the house in Cedar Rapids once their children were up and gone. "Honestly, Iris," Gladys had said to her from the door of the double walk-in closet in her bedroom not long after they moved. "You don't have to keep living in that little box up on cinder blocks. Roy must be doing all right." Gladys never let you forget how well Dale had done in what she called "electronics." What he was, was good at selling people TVs and dishwashers whether they needed them or not.

The time when it seemed like there was extra money passed quickly. First she had some trouble with her back that kept her in the doctor's office, then sharing the cost of Mama's care with Gladys, and bearing the whole bill for Roy's mother. Before she knew it, it was time to think small, to start her and Roy's retirement.

She took in the pictures of Trudy that lined the shelves two and three deep. She could look at Trudy at six months, at three, at five, and call her up, whole and perfect, voice and all. She still had all her little dresses and coats, saving them all these years for a granddaughter. When Halley came, Trudy did take the wicker bassinet, the pram. "I'm going to have a yard sale," Iris had threatened after Trudy produced her second boy, "make some room in my closets." But when Trudy didn't protest, she'd realized it was herself she'd be hurting. Even Trudy's high school dresses were here, the skirts on them no longer than a pair of short shorts. Trudy had made her hem each one until she could touch bare thighs with her fingertips.

In one of the last clippings Trudy had sent, there had been a picture of her wearing a lopsided square little sixties dress. Iris had gone to the closet in Trudy's room, ran her hands across the short skirts, wondering what memories Trudy had resurrected in her teenaged outfit. Trudy never looked at her old clothes. She had grown impatient the one time Iris suggested she take her old dresses, wear them on stage. "It's the idea of the dress, not the dress itself." And she had no interest in hearing how things were when she was coming up. "Don't tell me what happened," Trudy would say, cutting Iris off when she started with some story from Trudy's childhood. "I have it in my head the way I saw it at the time. I don't want to muddy that with someone else's impressions."

So Iris kept her stories for herself. Roy had no interest in them, he never had. She could remember him coming home, his legs and back aching from standing all day on concrete. She would start with some cute thing Trudy had done or said, and he would hold up his hand, point to the TV. "The news, Iris."

The Truda shrine, Phil had jokingly called Iris's house the one time he bothered to visit them. Truda, that's what she called herself now. She'd run up on the name when she studied German in college. "Truda means loved one," she'd said. "Trudy's nothing but a nickname."

"There were some people right here in town whose last name was Trudy," Iris said in her defense.

"Oh for God's sake, Mama. That's just some made up Ellis Island name."

Iris had no idea what Trudy was talking about but she nodded like she always did when her daughter's words confused her. Later, when she had the house to herself, she looked up Ellis Island in the World Book. Staring at the old photographs of European immigrants, Iris longed to tell Trudy how she had really chosen her name; that the feel of the word, in her mouth, on her lips, had seduced her. Instead she kept the secret for herself. She and Roy—who knew nothing more about her choice of names than Trudy did—were the only ones who called her Trudy anymore.

Iris's attention drifted to the picture of Halley and Samuel—one of the few she had of the two of them—on the end table by the couch. It was a small wonder Phil felt the way he did about her keeping Trudy's things. Those two never saved a single baby thing. Once Samuel finished with Halley's hand-me-downs and toys, they went to Goodwill. And they'd stopped taking baby pictures after Halley turned two and Samuel came along. There was the VCR, their Christmas present for her and Roy last year, and the tapes made on the children's birthdays. She'd tried watching them, but the camera had swung around, cutting off heads, recording the everyday noise of the coffee grinder, the TV, Trudy and Phil's arguments about where the camera should go next. Those tapes didn't make her feel any closer to her grandsons than she did to the people on that TV show. They weren't special like her photographs of Trudy, each one a moment she'd managed to hold back from time.

Unlike the clothes, Trudy wanted some of the pictures for herself. She planned on using them in her work for "imaging." Iris knew better than to ask the meaning of such things. If she did, Trudy would snap her tongue against her teeth and explain it the way she would to somebody who already understood what she was talking about. But Iris had seen the bulletin board that covered one wall of Trudy's studio, the pictures and newspaper clippings about murder, divorce, and parenting, all push-pinned side by side into the cork. At the center of the board was the picture of the Macon family reunion Iris had given her. Trudy had cut the photograph apart, rearranging bodies and heads, couplings. If the world made more sense maybe Roy's mother would have been a man, and if she were a man maybe she would have married her sister-in-law. But Trudy had put Roy off by himself and Iris was paired with Roy's younger brother, the Macon she'd first set her cap for. A slow fear settled over her.

Trudy saw through things without being told, and it frightened her to think her daughter might know things she didn't dare admit to herself.

Now before Trudy's visits she hid the snapshot albums, and counted the framed pictures before Trudy left. She'd be welcome to all of them when she was gone, nobody else would want them. Until then, they were her memories, put together the way she saw fit.

Q
JOHNSTON

As It Should Be . . .

Etta L. Worthington

I heard him say an evangelist would be there, in those tent meetings off Main Street on the empty lot that was Parsons Fruit Market before it burned down ten years ago. Everybody in town still referred to it as Parsons. I used to slip into the store to buy cigarettes when I had the money. It was only a mile from my house, which was convenient, since all the other stores were in the center of town. That meant at least two and a half miles of walking unless I was lucky enough to get a ride from my sister Florence. Since she didn't like smoking, I was scared to buy cigarettes when I was with her. But at Parsons I could buy cigarettes. Didn't matter what kind. I wasn't partial to one particular brand, although my husband, that scum, glad he's dead, always used to smoke Camels, so I made sure I never got those. Anyhow, they were too strong, so I'd go for a menthol cigarette and hope something was on sale, or if I was lucky I'd have enough for a carton and wouldn't have to go out for more for a long time.

"There'll be special music," he said. "On Tuesday night there's a choir coming all the way from Sioux City."

I didn't tell him I knew all about those choirs and singing in huge canvas tents with dirt and sawdust aisles and wooden folding chairs borrowed from the undertaker and sultry July evenings when the trees didn't move and you'd swear God forgot to breathe or else there would be some hint of breeze. But it didn't matter then. I was young and didn't mind the rivulets of sweat trickling down my face, pooling in the crevice between my breasts and rolling down my stomach and tickling me almost like Ben did when he'd run his hand over me later those nights back behind the tent under the willow trees where nobody could see. I didn't mind none because he was only two rows behind me and I knew that later I'd find a minute to sneak out there in the dark with him.

No, I didn't tell the preacher that. Not the kind of thing he'd be wanting to hear, but I must have been smiling some because he seemed more encouraged. He probably thought I was interested and in a way I was. I wanted to go, maybe just to remember, although this wasn't Mississippi and I didn't think they had revivals quite the same way up north. In fact, he didn't even mention the word revival. Everyone knew they're revivals. Why didn't he say so? They called them "special meetings" in Iowa.

"Can I give you a ride? You and your son, of course. He'll like the chalk talks," the preacher said. "There are wonderful chalk drawings done in the meetings that are given away to someone in the audience each night."

My son. I wondered how he knew I had a son since Elliott wasn't home at the time. Did the preacher know that he was an idiot? Did he know that from the moment of birth he was strange, not right, and that I had looked at him fresh from the womb and wished he would die like Mary Jo had, because his head was so fat and his eyes so spread-out, I knew on sight that he had no mind and I'd be regretting having him my whole life.

I wanted to tell the preacher, the boy's an idiot and no one would want him around. That was why I pretty much stayed away from people because no one liked to see an idiot, but all I said is, "He's retarded." That would shut him up, I thought, and he'd make a quick exit since all the other preachers had done that. He said he knew all about Elliott and I guessed he must be from the church that Florence had been going to. Must be she put him up to stopping by to talk, since how else would he have known about Elliott? She'd always been trying to get me to come.

He said, "We'd love to have you and Elliott attend. Elliott will like the chalk talk because it's pictures as well as words and who knows, maybe Elliott will be the lucky one to take home the illustration the chalk artist makes."

I knew Elliott would like that, so I said, "Yes."

He left, dropping in my hand a badly printed card telling the times for those special meetings and a bulletin from last Sunday's church service. I put them aside, although I knew I wouldn't read them ever and would wait a week or two before throwing them out.

It *was* Florence's church. I had half a mind to ring her up and ball her out for having that preacher call on me. But I'd never have the nerve to say anything bad to her because she's my older sister and practically raised me, what with being thirteen years older than me and with our mother being sick all the time. Besides, what would it hurt going to one tent meeting? Didn't mean I was going to join the church and I knew for sure they weren't going to get any money out of me. What with the money from Social Security for me and Elliott and the little bit from Sam's pension, I hardly made ends meet. I probably wouldn't have, if it weren't for the surplus food we got monthly from the government.

I was tired of it, though. Always came in plain brown wrappers or tin cans printed with big black block letters. The luncheon meat was supposed to be like Spam, but it wasn't a tenth as good and sort of greasy. The only way I could think of eating it was to smother it with a brown sugar glaze and bake it. Elliott liked that pretty good, and since the cans were big it would spread to two meals because I didn't eat much of it. The dried eggs came in cans too, and I tried to find ways to use them. First time I mixed them up just like it said to on the back. I added water and then cooked it up just like scrambled eggs. It was so bad neither one of us could eat very much of it, not even dousing it good with ketchup. I never tried that again. Now the only way I ever used it was in baking, for cakes. Or when I cooked pancakes for supper, which was at least once a week.

I was glad for most of the other food—the flour, corn meal, dry milk. Elliott liked to mix up the milk. Every time we needed more milk, I pulled down a big bowl from the top shelf of the kitchen cupboard and measured out the milk, then added the right amount of water and gave him a big spoon to stir it all up. It was impossible to get all the lumps out but I let him try for as long as it kept him entertained. Then after he finished, I got out the strainer and poured the milk through it and tried to push through any of the remaining lumps. Elliott didn't complain about drinking powdered milk, since it's just about as good as real milk when it's cold, only a little thinner.

I was not about to start giving money to any church. Ma used to make a big deal about tithing. Why she'd take the money Pa'd bring home, sometimes it'd be as little as ten dollars a week, and she'd put one dollar of that ten aside "to put in the collection," she'd say. She'd drop it in a tin can next to the cookie jar and whichever one of us kids was the best that week got to put it in the wicker basket they passed around at church. When my turn came, I'd figure out ways I could pretend to put it in the basket but really slip it up my sleeve instead. Ma kept such a sharp eye out that my plans never got past the scheming stage.

Didn't ever seem right, when I needed new shoes, to be putting that money in the basket, but she wouldn't hear of missing a Sunday contribution. I was pretty sure she gave more than the ten percent she said was the Lord's due.

The phone rang. It was Florence. "Would you like to come tonight to the special meetings?"

I said I was too tired but that the preacher'd been by and that I'd be there tomorrow night. I wondered whether the preacher was there in the background, putting her up to the call, but I didn't say anything because I didn't want to cause any ill will. Florence was my only close blood relative alive, except for Elliott, but he didn't count.

Six of us kids grew up in that household. I didn't know how me and her ended up being the heartiest ones, but all the rest died along the way.

I got good at funerals, since for a while there were so many of them. The one year Pa died and so did baby Mary Jo. And then it was Ma to go, then my brother Elwood and then Sam. Not much of anybody showed up at his funeral, even though he'd worked on the railroad all his life. Nobody really liked him and I didn't blame them none. I wasn't too sad when he died although I got out my black dress and worked up a few tears and practiced looking tired and worried.

Back then I was happy about it, 'cause I hoped I'd meet a man and get married again. By this time I knew that wouldn't happen. I had an idiot son and wasn't so young and pretty and didn't have money to spend on new dresses and makeup to make me look better. I figured I'd spend the rest of my days on Fourth Street in a tiny house, sitting and watching television and taking care of Elliott.

All day Tuesday I felt kind of excited. It'd been such a long time since I'd really been anywhere—anywhere at all—that even the thought of going to a tent meeting was stimulating. From early morning I mulled over what to wear, although all my dresses were of the same Arnel fabric and the shape of them was the same, too. I did have some cotton ones, but they were house dresses and I wouldn't ever think of wearing them out.

I told Elliott when I fed him supper, "We're going to a tent meeting at the church tonight."

I knew he didn't quite understand what I was talking about, but he didn't complain.

It took longer to get him dressed than I'd planned. I put him in his best pants and a white shirt. Since it was July, I decided a tie wasn't necessary. That barely left me time to dress and fix my hair and I felt half angry with him, sitting there, plugged into the television.

I was ready ahead of time even with having to get Elliott dressed, although I felt rushed. I chose my best summer dress and hoped it was not too ordinary looking.

A blue Chevy sedan pulled up in front of the house and the preacher himself got out to come to the door for us. I was a little nervous even though I'd rehearsed Elliott on how to say "how do you do" and "nice to meet you." Somehow I got through the introductions quite nicely and Elliott did just as I'd instructed him. I started to relax as I got in the car, where I sat up front between the preacher and Elliott.

"We have to pick up some more people. I hope you two won't mind being crowded into the front seat for a short while."

I did mind a little and leaned to the right as far as I could without being too obvious, because I didn't want to actually touch the preacher, although there was no way of totally avoiding contact. The warmth my hips felt indicated that his were close. I was quite uncomfortable with that, but there was no way to move away from him without totally scrunching Elliott up to the door. Who knew what he would say—Elliott didn't know when not to say inappropriate things—so I just hoped that it wasn't too far until we added the other riders and were on to the tent meeting.

The car turned left up Bremer County Road and try as I might, I couldn't keep myself from leaning as the car turned. I found my shoulders touching the preacher's and I pulled myself back as quickly as the car straightened out. I was embarrassed.

He must have been embarrassed too. He'd been talking since I got in the car, and even though Elliott and I didn't join in the conversation other than to say yes or no to his questions, he just kept right on. That must be the way preachers were. They did know how to talk. They could talk for an hour or so, and up in front of people. That amazed me because all I ever possibly could think of saying in front of a group of people would be about two sentences worth and then it wouldn't be loud enough for anyone to hear.

At five I made a fool of myself up in front of people for the first and last time. It was the Christmas program. I was supposed to say some Bible verse I had memorized, it probably wasn't more than ten words long. I had been rehearsed by my mother for days till I could practically say it in my sleep. When it came time for the program, I froze. It was only the platform of the storefront church my parents were members of. Probably there were no more than seventy-five people in the room, but looking out over the pews it seemed like hundreds and I forgot what I was supposed to say or when I was supposed to say it and so I started crying. Nothing could console me, so they hauled me off the platform. My mother took me in the back Sunday School room and tried to get me to stop. She was disappointed, I knew, after all her hard work and then me making a spectacle of myself, but they never again gave me a speaking part in the Christmas program. I didn't mind being a sheep or an angel or a wise man, as long as I didn't have to say any lines all by myself.

The car slowed, getting ready to pull up a lane. Suddenly I recognized it and I wanted to disappear into the floorboards of the car, or maybe just jump out of the car and run off into the woods, but Elliott was there and I couldn't get out of the car. Even if I did, I knew I wouldn't have the guts to run away. But I felt like I wanted to die.

How could he? Make me ride in the car with her! Oh, it had been years now, more years than I'd like to think. Fifteen must be, but it still felt fresh. That was when I first knew Sam was seeing her on the side. Everybody said she was just poor white trash and I had a few other names I could think of besides that. Over the years I'd managed to avoid running into her, after I learned about her and Sam, but I'd been dreading it.

The preacher said, "I'll just be a minute," and got out of the car. I wished I knew how to drive so I could back down the lane. That way I wouldn't have to lay eyes on her, let alone ride in the same car.

Betty Rand was the last person in the world I wanted to see. I knew the feelings I had at the thought of seeing her were not appropriate for going to church with but I couldn't help it, not after all that happened. I was relieved it wasn't Betty stepping down from those decaying stairs, but one of her daughters and two small children.

"I didn't know she had children," I mentioned to Elliott and he didn't reply. That was not unusual since when I talked to him I knew he didn't understand. Somehow it just felt better knowing that I was saying it to another human being, although I knew that he was only a half or a quarter of one, if one really got down to it.

What was her name? I'd known it, but it didn't come to mind. Fortunately the preacher got in and said, "Can I introduce you to Sarah Torrey?"

And I said, "Oh yes, I knew her mother."

I wanted to ask what was happening to her mother although I didn't really care but I wanted to know anyhow, and I seriously wished she were dead.

The preacher made some explanations. "Her mother's recently gotten out of the hospital. This is the first time Sarah is coming to our church," he said.

I glanced in the rear view mirror right in front of me, looked back, and nodded that, yes, I understood.

I didn't remember hearing where the two babies came from but I was sure she wasn't married. Betty had one other daughter, who was married but had no children. That must be her house. Must be the whole family's living there.

Of course, this *was* the kind to bring into a revival meeting, I told myself, sniffing out a possible conversion. I knew what that was like—that guilt before the storm—those heart-wrenching, soul-sobbing transformations.

I'd had lots of them when I was young. More times than I could remember, I had raised my hand, then found myself up at the front, kneeling at the altar rail, sobbing my eyes out and saying some kind of half-coherent prayer and confessing anything I thought of, although I never had anything that big to pray about. Then I'd ask Jesus to come into my heart again and save me, and I'd dry my tears and feel kind of tired and warm and comfortable like everything was all right again.

Florence told me that's all wrong, and I figured must be because of what she'd learned from this preacher. She said, "You can only get saved once and then you don't need to keep doing it over and over."

That made me kind of sad thinking about it, because it was so nice to feel saved.

"You can backslide," Florence said, "and just not live for the Lord at all, but that doesn't mean you lose your salvation."

I asked, "Does that mean you can get away with doing just about anything you please after you once get saved?"

Florence explained, "No, that's not the way it works, because someone who's really saved won't want to go out and live like the world and if they do, they must not really be saved."

"How do you really know?" I asked.

"If you're really saved you know it because you have the Holy Ghost living inside you and He tells you that you are really saved, so you don't have to worry when you do sin. You sometimes have to rededicate your life to the Lord if you backslide a little."

I figured that really meant the same thing as getting saved again, but I didn't want to argue with Florence, since she was older than me and she knew more Bible verses.

Maybe I'll get rededicated tonight, I told myself, as we came closer to the big mustard-colored canvas tent. I got hot just looking at the tent and I wondered if it'd feel any different than getting saved again. Then I worried about what Elliot'd do when I went forward and knelt at the altar. Maybe he'd come too and get saved. Wouldn't hurt him none, but I knew he wouldn't have the slightest idea what it was all about.

We drove up the lane to the tent, and I thought it looked good in the distance but as I got close, it looked dirty. I could almost smell the mildew and canvas. I was glad I went to the bathroom the last thing before I left the house and had Elliott go, too, because tents don't have bathroom facilities and we'd have to walk half a block to the Sinclair station to find a restroom.

The parking lot was rutted with small puddles from the day before's downpour. I grabbed Elliott's arm as I made my way from the car to the tent. Since he was as tall as me, he's good to balance on. I wore new white high heels which I tried not to get muddy. They weren't really new, just new to me since two weeks ago when I went to a rummage sale at St. Mary's in Oelwein. Florence took me and I bought myself another housedress and a pair of shoes that didn't fit bad and a new winter jacket for Elliott. He always lost his or somehow got it caught in something and then it would tear and he wouldn't wear it with holes in it. I didn't have a sewing machine so there wasn't much repairing I could do and I just had to find another shirt or jacket or pants if I could.

Sometimes I went to a secondhand store on Main Street in Oelwein too, but I never knew if there'd be anything good.

The preacher scurried off to do whatever preachers do just before a service starts. That woman's daughter chased after her two. They ran in different directions and I noticed one was dangerously close to jumping in a mud puddle but I averted my eyes and concentrated on not getting my new shoes muddy. But I felt a little guilty. Maybe I should have given her a hand with them.

Inside the tent, my eyes adjusted slowly to the dimness. Fortunately we arrived early enough to get a good choice of seats. Sitting in the back would call attention to myself and that was the last thing I wanted to do. I hoped people wouldn't notice there was a strange woman with an idiot son. I chose a seat off the middle aisle, a little over half the way from the platform.

I put Elliott next to me, on the aisle, and then pointed out the easel for the chalk talk. I told him, "The man's going to draw a very pretty picture so you better watch close. There'll be pretty lights on it too." He seemed interested.

I didn't know what he thought about most of the time. I wasn't even sure he if he could think. Could be he was like a dog or cat and just responded to things happening around him. Maybe it was easier on him that way. He was very simple and usually easy to please. Once the music started and the chalk talk, I was sure he'd be entertained.

The music did start although it was ten minutes before the service was to begin. They had an organ, as I figured, but not like the pump organs I used to have at my revivals. This one was electric. The tone was more even, but somehow I missed the pumping, throbbing sound that used to match the pumping throbbing feeling I'd have sitting in the choir. Waiting for Ben. Waiting for God. Waiting for something amazing and wonderful, I didn't really care if it was Ben or God.

The organist played a sort of quiet version of *Give Me that Oldtime Religion* and I wanted her to speed it up and get a beat in it, something to tap my foot to, but that never happened. The next piece was equally disappointing and I realized this wasn't going to be the same as it was in Mississippi.

The preacher came to the platform along with a man in a black suit, I assumed it was the evangelist, and a plump woman in a brown and gold dress. She must be the soloist and I didn't feel so bad about my clothes since her dress didn't look one speck better than mine although I noticed she was wearing a string of gold beads and matching earrings.

On the other side of the aisle, two rows up from where I sat, I spotted Jake Boyd and I almost laughed out loud, wondering what he was doing at a revival. Hard to think of Jake as a church-going sort, not from what I knew about him.

When we first moved to town, I went to D and J's Meat Market, and for as long as I went there, Jake had always been behind the counter, waiting on customers and making special cuts of meat to the customer's request. He was always friendly enough and just like I thought a butcher should be—big and burly and loud.

Never seemed like he paid any special attention to me until after Sam died. I didn't know if I was imagining it, at first. He started getting friendlier.

"Hi, Mrs. Bokum," he'd say every time I came in the shop.

"What's your first name?" he asked once. After that it was Ardis.

It was ever so slow and I didn't mind, having some extra attention when I came in the store. I swore he started giving me better cuts of meat and not charging a dime more. I didn't mind that. And I didn't know when it started but it seemed like he was quick to come out from behind the counter when I stopped in and always tried to get close to me. He'd steer me in a certain direction, take my arm and direct me to a display case and point out how good the chicken looked today, and what nice fat pork chops he had for sale. Often, he'd find a way to lean over me to point out something and I'd feel him hot and sweaty, smelling like meat and man, but I didn't think much of it.

One day, he whispered, "I have a surprise for you."

"What?" I asked.

"I saved some good big soup bones for you but my partner would be mad if I just gave them to you in the front of the other customers so you'll have to come around to the back in five minutes."

I wasn't about to pass up that offer. Thinking about what a hearty broth I'd cook up for me and Elliott and how long I could make it stretch, I crept around to the back of the store.

Glancing around nervously, he whisked me in the dark back entrance of the meat shop, and pulled me into a small side storage room that smelled of blood and meat. I looked around and wondered where the soup bones were.

"The bones," I said to him, "the bones."

"I have a bone for you," he said, getting unbearably close and I smelled sweat and pipe tobacco on him and it dawned on me that he wasn't talking about the soup bone. I wanted to scream but he grabbed my arm and pulled me to him. I didn't scream, but I pulled away and rushed out of the room, stumbling on the threshold and crashing into a broom and mop next to the exit.

I must have run at least three blocks before I stopped. I ran till my chest ached, till I could hardly breathe. I was scared to look back, thinking he might be running after me, red-faced and jowly, puffing and reaching for me.

Later I discovered he had a reputation for this kind of thing. I was embarrassed to have been taken in by him. I stopped going to the shop and from then on I only bought meat from the Shur Fine grocery even though I knew the cuts weren't as good. I dreamed of him for months. I was always running away from him, and he was chasing me, all red-faced and fat. As he was gaining on me, I'd always stumble, and then I'd hear his zipper sliding down.

Now here he was in a revival service. I remembered hearing from Florence that he was a member of the church. I wondered if he still lured widows into his back room.

I shouldn't have been surprised, but somehow I was. I expected people in the church to be different, to be somehow less base, more than human perhaps. Not sure why I expected that, because it had never been that way. For as long as I remembered going to church, I heard gossip about so and so and who they were having an affair with, or stumbled on an illicit meeting in a back hall. Maybe they were all like that, I thought, and looked over the congregation speculating on who's having affairs with whom.

The singing started and I couldn't concentrate on my speculations anymore so I started singing *There is a Fountain Filled with Blood*. I didn't even have to look at the hymnbook I held for Elliott, because I knew every word of all five verses. Elliott obediently held one end of the book and looked at it, but since he couldn't read much, he didn't sing along.

He'd always liked music, from when he was a tiny baby. I remembered holding him, rocking him when he was colicky. And I'd rock and rock and sing "lullaby and good night" or maybe "rock a bye baby in the tree top." He was so warm and sweet and soft that I was always shocked when I looked at his broad flat face that seemed so ugly, so unlike the cuddly soft baby I rocked in my fantasies. But he always smiled and cooed when I had finally lullabied his crying away, so I'd forget that he wasn't quite right. It didn't matter that he didn't look right, or was so slow in trying to talk, or crawl or walk.

I'd been lucky, really, come to think of it. He was pretty easy to manage, even though he was nearly a man in size. I'd heard about some retarded children with a mean streak in them. I didn't know how I'd ever tolerate that. I heard of a woman over in Waverly with this daughter who's retarded too. She learned to swear somehow, and whenever she was unhappy, she'd just shout out an oath wherever she was, didn't matter if it was in church or in the grocery store. She took to hitting her teachers and throwing things in school, till they finally asked her not to come anymore. The mother had to put her in an institution where they take care of retarded and mentally ill people. She only came home for weekends once or twice a year.

Elliott will never go to some kind of home, I told myself, not as long as I'm healthy enough to care for him. I chose not to think about old age and what it would be like then. I couldn't stand to see him pushed around and treated like an animal, ushered here or there, penned in, tied down or whatever. Some of those places put people in strait jackets every night, even if they're no bother.

I heard that from Millie Clark who lived a few doors down from me. She used to work at Independence as a maid and had wild tales to tell. Since she worked there I figured they must be true but Florence always told me to pay no mind to Millie.

She was the one who told me about Barbara Benton being sent to Independence. I really never knew Barbara more than seeing her at the store, but her husband Lester drove the schoolbus Elliott took to school every day.

"Barbara was going around threatening Lester with knives, even took a knick out of one of his ears, and that's why he committed her," Millie reported.

Far as I knew she's still there. Millie said, "All she does is rock in her chair all day and complain of little black bugs bothering her."

I felt sorry for Lester, and noticed him in the back of the tent setting up another row of chairs for latecomers. I made a note to speak to him after the meeting. He'd always been kind to Elliott and made sure the others on the bus didn't give Elliott too hard of a time.

I wasn't sure what to do when Elliott got too old for school. They had a special education program for up to age nineteen so I had little more than two years left. Elliott liked it, I thought. He liked me packing him the big black lunchbox that his father used to take on the railroad and filling his thermos with milk. And he brought home papers of the work he did and was very proud of them.

He didn't go to school in town but took the bus there and then another one to Oelwein for classes. Thirty miles of riding on a bus a day. But I'd visited his class and there were others just like him, and everybody seemed to get along well, so I figured he was happy, and he was learning something. He always wanted to play with money and put it in different piles and I thought they taught them at school how to count it so I tried to get him to count up the piles but he got confused over nickles and pennies and how many pennies in a nickel and so forth, and I wasn't very patient so I gave up and just let him play with them.

Would you be free from your burden of sin, the audience sang. I sang along too, and though I figured I should be guilty on some count or other, I couldn't quite feel burdened down by sin. I was getting too old to do very much sinning. Now back when I was young, yes, yes, I might have had reason.

There were more than Ben, although he was the biggest reason. Other boys noticed me too. But it was Ben I really loved. Ben that I ached for. Ben whose eyes made me melt. Ben whose lips made me forget what my mother told me not to let any boy do to me. And it was Ben who went away to join the Navy and never wrote like he promised, and who came home months later on leave with a city girl on his arm. And something in me died then.

The other boys who paid attention to me, well, I pretended I liked them for as long as it entertained me. And I'd let them kiss me or maybe run their hands up under my blouse or my skirt, but I never really felt anything deep inside. Not like with Ben. Most of the time I couldn't stand them, after they'd been touching me, and I just wanted to go home and take a bath. My mother wondered out loud about how clean I'd gotten, always wanting to bathe.

"You'll dry your skin out. And you take entirely too much time in the bathroom when there are other people needing to use it," she complained.

I didn't recall their names or their faces. But I couldn't forget their sweat, the heat of their bodies, the way they'd tremble a little once I let them start feeling me up. And their breathing. It was heavy and coarse and loud, and not much different than Jake Boyd's, and maybe that was why he made me feel nauseated. So much like all those boys whose bodies I grew to hate, mostly because they weren't Ben and never would be Ben.

But sin? I wasn't exactly sure what it was anymore. Funny about that. When I was young everything was quite clear. Things were either this or that, and as I got older I forgot which was which and everything got muddy. It was nicer that way. I eliminated cigarettes from the sin category. It was neither good or bad. That was about the only little pleasure I had other than drinking a little wine around holidays, which I figured I deserved as well. I probably would have drunk wine a little more often than that, if it wasn't so expensive.

Florence wouldn't approve for sure, and I thought she'd say something about it. It wasn't surprising since Ma was that way. She had no tolerance for alcohol. Probably 'cause her father took to liquor when he was a young man, and drank himself all around the South, turning up at home infrequently. Drink took him to an early grave, too. Or at least that's always what she told the whole lot of us, and since we never knew our grandpa or grandma, there was no questioning her facts.

I didn't know how many times I heard her say, "I don't ever want to hear tell that any of my children even as much as put a bottle to their lips."

I figured she'd die right on the spot if she ever caught me trying it, although I knew for sure that my brother Ned had drunk moonshine on more than one occasion.

I never tried it when I lived at home. I was too scared. Too sure some demon was going to leap out of the bottle and make me prisoner to it, right after the first drink. It came as quite a surprise to me, after I was married, that wine tasted good and sweet, and made me felt light and happy.

I made sure whenever Ma visited I hid the bottles. It wasn't that I drank very much at all but Sam liked to have his whiskey. He liked it after a long hard day at the yards. I never understood how he could stand the taste of it, but he did. He'd grumble and threaten to take off when Ma would come, but ultimately he'd tolerate a few days without his whiskey bottle out next to where he sat on the couch, just so she wouldn't know I had alcohol in the house.

I tried to keep it from Florence as well, but I knew she'd seen Sam sitting with his whiskey and ice some nights when she'd stop over. But she'd never seen me drinking wine.

Elliott nudged me, smiling. A ventriloquist. I could have predicted that. A dummy. Like what sat next to me. I told him what to say and he said it, and I told him what to do and he did it. The only difference was that one didn't have to help a dummy dress every day, or make sure he had his lunch pail in hand when he went out to meet the bus.

I didn't listen to the ventriloquist because his jokes were stale and I was sure he'd end up giving a little sermon intended to steer the boys and girls in the right direction.

Suddenly I wanted to get up and rush to the back of the tent. I wanted to up and leave. I was nineteen again and I'd just found out that Ben loved someone else, and I couldn't stand singing in the choir or any more sermons about being sure you were saved, and serving the Lord and doing God's will. No, I was nineteen again, and Ben didn't love me and I was sure it was because I listened too long and hard when they talked to girls about how a fellow has to respect you, and saving yourself for marriage, and that's what I'd done. And even though Ben had just about touched every inch of my body, I'd never actually let him do that, even though he wanted to and kept trying to get me to say yes, but I was afraid. Of what, I wasn't sure. But just afraid, so I never did it. But I was nineteen and he was back with a girl on his arm and I was sure they were doing *that*, and I thought if only I'd let him do *that*, things would be different. And I wanted to leave that holy congregation and go out and offer myself to the first man in a khaki uniform that passed my way, and never go back. But I stayed.

And so I also stayed in the tent on the old Parsons Fruit Market grounds. Because I realized I wasn't nineteen, and there was nothing exciting and wonderful and dangerous out there to run to. And while being inside was boring, it was also warm and safe. So I stayed.

I couldn't go. I had this boy, this idiot man-child, who sat next to me, and what would he do if I left? And I'd have to walk home all the way. I knew the preacher would come by looking for some explanation for my quick exit, pretty sure I was under conviction. I knew he'd be ready to zero in on me, pouncing for a conversion.

Safe, I stayed. Too tired even to feel angry or trapped. Just safe, and sleepy, and nearly dead. It was tiring now when I thought of Ben. I got all worked up for a minute, but then the energy drained out of me and I felt lethargic. And so old.

The choir was nowhere near as good as the one I was in. I heard them start on

Just a closer walk with thee

Grant it Jesus this my plea ...

I smiled, discovering there must be a Mrs. Richards in this choir, too. My Mrs. Richards sat in the row right behind me. I didn't know how I could possibly stand listening to her nasal warbling. She hit the right note okay, but her voice stuck out like a sore thumb.

"Blend," Mrs. Peel the choir director yelled out during rehearsals. "Listen to your neighbor and blend in."

I was sure she said it so often on account of Mrs. Richards, but it never changed the way she sang. Everyone was relieved when she went to visit her daughter in Texas for several weeks every year. I suspected Mrs. Peel felt the same way and I noticed she planned the nicest pieces to do on those Sundays Mrs. Richards was gone.

I wondered, listening to this choir, whether their Mrs. Richards was as old as mine was, and whether she ate as much garlic. At times I wasn't sure whether it was her irritating voice or the aroma of garlic mixed with body odor that bothered me the most. It was a relief when Mrs. Peel decided they needed another alto, and I was permanently separated from Mrs. Richards. That's when I got closer to Ben, which made choir wonderful.

If at all possible, I positioned myself right in front of him, knowing that he'd prop his knees on the rung of my chair in such a way that his legs would be touching my rear end. Or when he got brave, he'd reach down to pick up his Bible under my chair and lightly run his hand over where his legs had been pressing. Oh heaven.

Now the chalk artist. The evening was never going to end. Not even to the message yet. I knew how these can go on and on, 'specially if the evangelist got wound up and heard enough "amens" from the audience.

As expected, the chalk artist created a beautiful sunset scene and talked while doing it and in the end turned on lights to highlight it. The only thing unexpected was that the chalk artist was a woman—the evangelist's wife. She drew quickly and surely and talked with a voice medium in pitch and easy to listen to.

She tied in concern about the day ending, and how that people never knew when their last opportunity was to accept Jesus Christ as Savior. The sunset was beautiful but of course unreal. As expected, somehow the preacher had rigged it so that Elliott got to take the chalk drawing home. He made a big deal about drawing from a basket the row and seat number. Yes, it was row twenty-six, left, seat one.

The preacher asked who had that seat, please raise their hand, and the usher came up and nudged Elliott. I told him, "Raise your hand." I told him he was going to get the drawing, so he did raise his hand.

"You can take the drawing home," I said and he beamed. The preacher asked him to come up after the service and claim his prize, and I whispered to Elliott that he'd go up after the service, and he nodded as if he understood.

Why Elliott, I wondered? Why did the preacher choose him to win the drawing? The small amount that I might contribute to the collection would be inconsequential, for certain.

The preacher was younger than me, by at least a couple of years. Or at least I thought so, although he had a daughter away at college, so perhaps he was my age. It all depended on when he got married.

His wife—I'd never met her but I've heard lots about her—she sat in the front with one of their children and wore a broad-brimmed straw hat decorated with a swatch of summer garden flowers.

I heard from Florence that she was quite the dresser and always seemed to find some way to put together the most interesting accessories. I'd heard more than that, too. Seemed that she was hot tempered, and didn't always get along with her husband. There had been several unanticipated leaves of absence, in which suddenly she had gone to visit her mother or brother for a week or two at a time. Most everyone figured it was because she wasn't getting her way—either in the church or with the preacher. Strange, I thought to myself. He seemed so in charge when he was up front.

I wondered if he was a better preacher than the evangelist. There were no amens from the audience—they seemed to avoid displays like that up north—and as the evangelist spoke, he rarely raised his voice at all. I found myself daydreaming and suddenly the organ started to play and everyone stood up and grabbed the hymnbooks on the ground and under their chairs. I might have even dozed, I didn't know for sure.

Just As I Am. I didn't need the hymnbook. I had sung that song hundreds of times. Hundreds. Sometimes I had sung the song through two or three times in a row until someone finally came forward.

The evangelist asked those who raised their hand to accept Christ as their Savior to come forward as the song was sung. I had dozed. I didn't remember the prayer and the pleading for individuals to make a decision for Christ.

No one budged on the first verse, and the organ played a soft interlude while the evangelist pleaded with those unnamed but by now embarrassed people who had raised their hands. "Come forward," he told them. "Don't put it off. You can go home tonight and know you're on the way to heaven. All you have to do is to come forward and we'll pray together."

A little girl of five or six went forward, and the evangelist went and put his arm around her. The song continued. I looked down at the hymnbook to predict how many minutes it would take to get through the next three verses. I felt a slight movement next to me and I realized Elliott was into the aisle and starting down it. He must have thought the preacher wanted him to come up there to get his drawing now instead of after the service.

If I'd been paying attention I could have caught him before he got out of the row, but it was too late. I couldn't run out into the aisle and pull him back. Everyone would see. And they wouldn't understand.

"Praise the Lord," the evangelist said at the end of the second verse. By now there were three children and Elliott in the front.

"But how about you?" he said. "You've been saved but you've gotten far away from the Lord. And you know tonight that He wants you to come back. He's just waiting there with open arms to welcome you just like the prodigal son. Won't you come forward tonight and tell Him that you want to live for Him again? Come as we sing the third verse."

Something tugged at the inside of me. It was the idea of someone standing with open arms. Of course I knew God didn't have arms, or at least I'd never been able to feel them, so I put that itch to go forward down, although if I went up I could make sure they didn't take very much time with Elliott. Surely they'd realize he couldn't understand.

Should I have followed him up there, and of course be forced into some sort of spiritual decision? Perhaps it was time to give my life to Christ again. I decided, no, no. If I did that they'd be hovering over me like yellow jackets in the fall. Yes, they'd be after me to join the choir, or teach Sunday School or help with Vacation Bible School. They got Florence, who never liked getting up in front of people and wouldn't make it as a teacher, to help out with their missionary society.

I asked her what they do.

"It's a monthly meeting," she explained. "We read letters from missionaries and pray for them. And after that we work on special projects for missionaries."

"Such as what?" I wanted to know.

"Well, things like making bookmarks or knitting mittens. And we collect old sheets and cut them into strips and roll them up so they can be used to bandage people," Florence said.

"Where do these things go?" I asked.

Florence said she thought the bandages went somewhere in Africa, maybe the Belgian Congo. And the little notebooks, which were made from the bright colored fronts of Christmas cards with sheets of blank white paper stapled to them—these were mailed to Africa too, she thought. She knew for sure the mittens were sent to an Indian reservation in New Mexico, because they'd just had a missionary come. He had told them about how many children were cold and not dressed warmly enough in winter.

Florence tried, degenerative arthritis and all, to knit mittens, but she must not have done very well because I hadn't noticed any more balls of yarn at her house. Her hands were too crippled to do that kind of work, but she always tried.

I didn't want to get that involved and I decided I'd let Elliott fend for himself. Or maybe I'd let them figure out how to get through to him. No, I stood at my seat all the way through *Just As I Am* and waited until the service had ended. Then I slowly made my way to the front to collect my newly saved Elliott. I saw him kneeling now at the front altar rail. The evangelist had his hand on his head and talked to him most earnestly.

I suppose that meant I'd have to take him to church with some regularity. Maybe the preacher would give us a ride Sundays, and that wouldn't be so bad. Maybe Elliott made a good choice after all.

I felt a little foolish standing there after the meeting had ended. Everyone else ambled towards the back of the tent, ready to go to their cars, or stood about in clumps, and chatted and laughed softly. I was painfully conscious of being alone and remembered Ruthie Adam's birthday party I was invited to when I was ten. Just thinking about going to her house made me so excited I hardly slept for two days before that Saturday afternoon affair. I didn't remember the cake or the presents or games, just those achingly long minutes that crept by. Those minutes when Ruth and her friends talked and laughed, and I, who knew none of them other than Ruth, was on the side, on the fringes, ever so quiet. I felt like I wanted to silently disappear.

There were people here whose names I knew, of course. It was too small a town to be unaware of other inhabitants even if I didn't know them personally. But it didn't seem right to go up and talk with them since I wasn't sure if they had any idea of who I was.

And I … I knew who I was. I was Ardis, the reprobate, who had resisted going forward. I was Ardis, the girl who used to neck under the trees behind the church. I was Ardis, the woman who snuck brandy into her house at Christmas, and smoked cigarettes on the sly. I was Ardis, mother of an idiot son. I was Ardis, mother of the newly converted idiot son.

The preacher came toward me, looking most serious.

Oh no, I said to myself, he's going to try to wring some sort of decision out of me. I panicked, just as I had in the car earlier that evening. Again the fantasy of streaking from the tent flickered through my mind. A harmless fantasy since I'd never been one to do things that draw attention to myself.

He was almost to me when I noticed his hands were full.

"Here's the drawing," he said. "I wanted to make sure Elliott got his drawing in good shape." Then he handed me the rolled up chalk drawing.

"The artist sprayed it with something so you won't get chalk on your hands if you happen to touch it. It would look lovely in a frame, don't you think?"

I agreed, although I hadn't thought of doing more than taping it to the wall in Elliott's bedroom. The wallpaper was quite old and stained from an old leak in the roof. This would cover it nicely.

He shuffled back down the aisle, slightly hunched and worried looking. "I'll be able to give you a ride home in about fifteen minutes," he promised.

I never had driven a car, so I'd gotten used to waiting for other people. I started going down the aisle, having spotted where Elliott sat with the evangelist's wife.

"Ellicott has accepted the Lord as his personal Savior," she reported happily.

I wanted to tell her that his name is Elliott, not Ellicott, but she didn't stop talking.

"He's asked Jesus to take away all his sins."

I wanted to ask her, what sins? Do idiots sin? They knew so little, how would they know to sin?

"You know, it's important that you bring the boy to church and Sunday School every week and read the Bible to him. Why, he has so much to learn about Jesus."

Elliott beamed. For a moment I thought he'd had a true religious experience. Like Moses' face that shone so brightly after he'd talked to Jehovah.

I realized it was no different than how he beamed when I visited his school and the teacher said how good he'd been. He just soaked up the attention. No transformation. No suddenly new Elliott. No Elliott now with a spark from God that had created life in that small round head of his. No Elliott who could suddenly speak and act like an adult. No Elliott who could now dress himself and wash behind his ears and cut his toenails. No. No miracle had happened. But he was smiling.

"I have your picture," I told him and he wanted to see it so I unrolled it and noticed that it looked much rougher up close. Somehow the magic of that sunset was lost when I wasn't at least twenty-five feet away with a nice colored light aimed at the horizon. But I was sure he wouldn't notice. He was happy. He'd like it in his bedroom.

"I'll put it up tomorrow," I promised him.

He beamed even more.

The lady was still there and she wanted me to fill out a form with name and address.

"The pastor knows who we are and where we live," I told her. "He brought us here tonight."

Then there was a call for hands to redistribute hymnbooks and someone roped Elliott into helping. I didn't think he understood that every third chair got a maroon hymnbook, but he went off happily to help. And I was left with her.

"Do you attend church and Sunday School regularly?" the evangelist's wife asked.

I admitted that no, I didn't.

"It's important that Ellicott attend church regularly. It's up to you to make sure that happens. By the way, have you been saved?"

"Oh yes," I assured her. I felt myself edging away from her. I wasn't anxious to share my religious history.

She said, "Praise the Lord. You must be very happy that he's accepted the Lord tonight."

There was nothing I could do but say yes. But then I had to add, "But you know that he's, he's . . . slow."

"Yes," she told me. "I know. But how wonderful that Jesus loves him just as much as any other child. When Jesus said let the little children come unto me, he didn't differentiate at all about their intellect. Jesus loves Ellicott very much. And it's so wonderful that he's discovered that tonight."

Wonderful? An odd term connected to Elliott. And I wanted to ask her if Jesus loved Elliott so much then why did children in school still make fun of him? And why was it so hard to take care of him? And if he was so loved and God did miracles, how come God didn't come down and transform Elliott's brain?

These questions, which brimmed near the surface of my mind, I knew I could never ask.

"Will we see you here tomorrow night?" she wanted to know.

I didn't answer immediately, and as if on cue the preacher appeared and said, yes, he'd be quite willing to pick me up tomorrow night at the same time and all I could do was nod my head yes, yes, as if I was part of a stream that was flowing smooth but strong down a river channel. Yes, yes, I would be there with Elliott tomorrow night, and somehow I knew that my nodding had committed me to a lot more.

Contributors

Marianne Abel works as a freelance editor and writer on the livestock and grain farm she owns and operates with her husband in rural Cedar Falls, Iowa. She has edited the award-winning quarterly *Iowa Woman* since 1990, and has published her essays and feature articles nationally.

Jo Ann Hendricks Bahr graduated from the University of Iowa with an emphasis in drawing, printmaking, and photography. An author and illustrator of a children's book, a storyteller, and a second-generation road woman, she makes her home in Webster City, Iowa.

Judith Bell grew up in Asheboro, North Carolina, and now lives in Arlington, Virginia, with her husband and son. She won the 1989 Washington Prize for Fiction for her novel *Real Love,* and has placed as a finalist in several fiction contests. Her stories have appeared in *First for Women, The Washington Review, Short Fiction by Women, Snake Nation Review,* and *The Washington College Review.* An art historian, she writes on the arts for *Art and Antiques, Elle, Omni, USAir,* and other magazines.

Hope Burwell lives with her lover of a dozen years on a middle-sized farm in northeast Iowa where they garden, make hay, and let cows and chickens live until they die natural deaths. She teaches writing, literature, and women's studies at Kirkwood Community College in Cedar Rapids. Like Joan Didion, she spends her "most passionate hours arranging words on paper." Burwell thinks of her writing-self primarily as an essayist. She has published essays in markets as varied as *The Des Moines Register, Iowa Woman, Ms.,* and the anthology, *One Teacher in Ten.* "Farm Wives" is her first short story.

Rose Hamilton-Gottlieb is a native Iowan who has lived in Orange County, California, for many years. She earned English and American Studies degrees from Cal State Fullerton, and has taught history and American Studies part-time in the California State University system for five years. Now she devotes all her time to writing fiction. The family farm where she grew up, near Casey, Iowa, provides the setting for "Forty Acres," which is derived from a chapter of a novel-in-progress called *The Hartin Place*. Three other chapters have been published as short stories in *The Elephant Ear*. Another short story, "The Suspect," appeared in *Room of One's Own* in 1993.

A. C. Peters is finishing an M.F.A. in Writing at Vermont College and is working on a novel about Southeast Asian refugees at her home in Mankato, Minnesota. Her poetry has appeared in *Mankato Poetry Review*. She has worked as a nurse with the developmentally disabled, and has taught college composition in Minnesota.

Lisa Phillips is a writer and public radio news producer in Fort Dodge, Iowa. A native of Connecticut, she studied English and Creative Writing at Oberlin College in Ohio. She has published fiction in *Plum Creek Review* and *Fiction Forum*, and won second place in the 1992 Mimi Zanger Fiction Competition. She has written interviews and articles for *Iowa Woman* and *Twist-n-Shout*. Her radio reporting has been aired on National Public Radio, Pacifica, Fifty-One Percent, and Native American News.

Patricia Stevens, a graduate of the Iowa Writers' Workshop, is a fiction writer and essayist in Iowa City, Iowa. She has been a Michener Fellow and a Nelson Algren Award winner. Ms. Stevens has recently completed a novel and is currently working on a fiction collection.

Etta L. Worthington lives in Oak Park, Illinois, where she works as the editor and publisher of *River Oak Review*. She has published poetry and short fiction, and recently completed a collection of short stories, *Sufferin' Saints*, and a novel, *Their Teeth on Edge*. Her play, "Just Another Decoration Day" was produced at the Paul Mellon Arts Center at Choate Rosemary Hall in 1994.